GRAVEL

REVENGE

LACTON

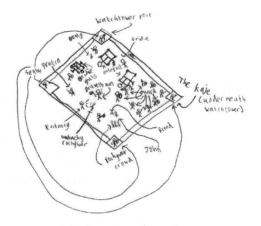

Benjamin Fun

Books in the series

Delton Guardians

Gravelburn's Revenge

The Espinox Trials

Gravelburn's

Revenge

Contents

Prologue

They sat by the fire, warming their hands. Well, technically John couldn't warm his hands because he was no longer alive. Gravelburn, the one made of stone, had been on the run for three days. He had broken out of his prison cell a few months after he had been captured by the members of Shock Unit (now called Power Unit) and imprisoned in their Delton base.

'Stone warriors don't eat,' thought Gravelburn bitterly, 'and neither do ghosts.' He wasn't really making much sense, but was just finding things to be unhappy about. He would have thought 'grass grows' or 'the wind blows' in the most venomous tone. He was miserable not because he was hungry, but because the enormous army he had once commanded had been greatly reduced in number by the Guardians, with most remaining survivors now mostly stuck in cave tunnels with the exits blocked. Gravelburn, former leader of the mighty Rochgwar army, was now merely leader of his travelling companions.

John was fine, although he wasn't too happy about losing his body. He floated around like a white mist and was still trying to get used to his new existence.

Suddenly, a rustling sound came from among the bushes. A mini Rochgwar popped out with an armful of twigs and proceeded to throw some onto the fire to keep it going.

'What took you so long?' chided Gravelburn.

'Don't be so harsh on him,' advised John. 'After all, he helped you escape.'

'Yes,' grumbled Gravelburn, 'I suppose you're right.' He paused for a few moments, deep in thought.

'And if it wasn't for him,' John added, 'you would still be playing I-Spy with that Nitro guy!'

'Yes,' snapped Gravelburn, 'but if it wasn't for me, he'd be stuck in an owl's nest, learning how to flap his arms and lift his massive body off the ground! And anyway, leave me alone in peace, you two. I'm thinking of more important things.'

Gravelburn scoffed at how things had turned out. He was not really thinking about important things but reminiscing about the great distant past, thinking of what might have been. He'd had a plan so evil it could wipe out anything that stood in its way, but the Delton Guardians had stopped it. This is a summary of what had happened so far: Rochgwars can regenerate from pieces of broken rock. Gravelburn had kept sending his men into battle, and while it looked like they were always losing, being smashed to pieces by the Delton Guardians, he was only biding his time, waiting for the day the broken pieces of rock would reform back into Rochgwars, overwhelm the Guardians in number and take over their base. His plan had been to repeat the strategy and move on to take over other Guardian bases. Over time he would have control of all the land, if things went to plan.

Shock Unit, as the group of young Delton Guardians was known then, had gone into the tunnels that Gravelburn's Rochgwars often used, and further on towards the Rochgwar camp, wiping out the stone warriors. They had defeated his army until only Gravelburn himself was left, and he soon found himself captured and a prisoner in Delton. Months passed with no end in sight for him, until he escaped with the help of John and Monty – the mini Rochgwar we mentioned earlier. (Where Monty had been during the battle and how he came about is a mystery to all.)

They were now headed for the outskirts of Delton, to escape being hunted down and re-captured, and to find someone or something to help them in their quest for world domination.

The fire that Monty kept feeding eventually died out overnight, but Gravelburn's thirst for revenge continued to burn deeply within him.

The Hunt

'Charge!' roared Slick, and Attack Unit ran forward. This unit was driving out the last remaining stone warriors from around their base. These pockets of Rochgwars had regenerated from broken rocks left around Delton after the last battle. Guardians had gone around breaking up bigger rock pieces in the weeks after the last battle, but must have overlooked a few. Suddenly Attack Unit, which was under Slick's command, tripped over obstacles while pursuing their enemies through the long grass. Well, actually it was Stealth Unit led by Ember that they tripped over. Stealth Unit had been practising their camouflage on a training exercise and had somehow gotten in the way of Attack Unit chasing down Rochgwars.

'Whoops! Sorry about that!' apologised Ember to Slick, as the Rochgwars slipped further away from their pursuers.

'After them!' commanded Slick.

The two units gave chase, but the Rochgwars were too fast for them.

'We'll have to give up!' wheezed Ember a while later after giving chase unsuccessfully.

'Too right!' said Slick, also out of breath. Their armour weighed them down. The two unit commanders had resigned themselves to the fact that the Rochgwars were going to escape, but suddenly, out of the blue, the outlines of the Power Unit leaders and their troops could be seen in the horizon!

The stone warriors who had escaped from Ember and Slick were shouting insults back at them, but they didn't see Cut, Fil, Nitro, Robin, Jack and Heath approaching from ahead of them.

'Bye!' shouted a stone warrior, waving back to Slick and Ember before he promptly ran into a collection of maces, swords, spears and lances and crumbled into a pile of rocks. His companions stood stunned and silent, and were quickly surrounded.

'Right,' said Robin to his troops. 'Herd these prisoners back to base to be dealt with. We'll join you in a bit. Lieutenant Azer, I'm putting you in charge of the prisoners. Now go!'

'Yes sir!' came the reply, and with that the soldiers left, leaving only the eight members of Power Unit behind. Power Unit was the new name given to the command group of the old Shock Unit, to show that each member was now part of an elite group and also in command of their own unit.

'Right guys!' said Robin. 'Gather around me. I have an urgent message from Murx Espin you all need to hear.'

They all gathered round as Robin produced a note. 'This is something Murx Espin received yesterday from one of our scouts,' he said, and read out:

General Espin,

There is not much time! Gravelburn has been spotted in Greenwood. Please send reinforcements to help track him down.

13

Robin looked up from the note to study the reactions of his friends.

'Is that it?' asked Slick. He had been expecting more.

Robin explained the situation. 'Murx Espin has decided that Power Unit should go and track Gravelburn down. It is important we catch him within the next few days, because the longer we wait, the more possible routes we have to cover, and the greater his chances of escape.

'It was thought that Gravelburn would head back to the tunnels to free his troops, but this latest message suggests he is actually making his way in the opposite direction through Greenwood. Sneaky devil. More cunning than a quick brown fox, our old adversary. He is trying to catch us off-guard by doing the opposite of what we expect him to do. What he is doing, heading through Greenwood, no one knows, but Murx Espin thinks the eight of us have the experience to track him down, and that we can move more swiftly on our own and without our units. So those are our latest orders, and that is our mission. We must move swiftly and make up the ground on Gravelburn. Move fast, don't pause unnecessarily, hunt him down.'

Tactics

Meanwhile, Gravelburn, John and Monty were on the move, and Gravelburn was still in an irritable mood. They encountered wet, muddy ground. But Gravelburn didn't want to get his feet wet or dirty again, so he ordered the Rochgwar minion to carry him across the bog. John thought Gravelburn was very lazy, but he never said it out loud, of course. John also knew that Monty the minion was thinking the same. But what was Gravelburn thinking? He thought that as the leader of Rochgwars, he was entitled to be carried across. He imagined that after he had eventually defeated the Delton Guardians, he would be carried around everywhere he went on a throne by four Rochgwars, and what was even better, he would have little Rochgwars throwing stones at him! (Rocks were like confetti to him.)

After they had crossed the muddy ground and the minion had set Gravelburn down, John turned to the latter and asked, 'So, Gravelburn, can you explain your plan to me one more time? There were some details that I couldn't quite understand.'

Gravelburn groaned. This was the third time since he had escaped that he had been asked to repeat his scheme. It wasn't just John's body that was hollow, his brain was hollow too. 'When we emerge out from the boundaries of this forest, there is a path that splits; the minion will go one way, and the two of us will go the other way to try to throw off any pursuing Guardians,' he explained yet again.

'But when the Guardians come to the fork in this road, they will know which way we have gone, won't they?' asked John. 'You know, because there will be two sets of footprints on one track – ours – and one set on the other. They will easily know which way we have gone!'

'Argh!' shrieked Gravelburn with frustration, hands by the side of his face. 'Remember, John, you are now a ghost! You don't leave footprints!'

'Don't remind me!' retorted John. He had suddenly remembered he was no longer human. He looked sullen for a while.

'As I was saying,' continued Gravelburn moments later, 'since you are a ghost, you do not make any footprints. Therefore there will only be one set of footprints on both paths. Then we shall all meet up at our objective. And whichever path the Guardians choose, they shall all eventually be crushed! Nobody can fully understand it at this time, but Gravelburn is always … one step ahead!'

All the time, while Gravelburn was explaining his plan, he was sketching it out on the wet muddy ground. It looked something like this:

*   *   *

Power Unit kept pushing forward as fast as they could. Robin realised they had to make up ground on the escaping Gravelburn, but at the same time he did not want to tire out his team such that when they got to

Gravelburn, they would be unable to subdue him. So they quick-marched for three hundred paces, then marched at a normal pace for the next two hundred paces, repeating this countless times. Robin monitored the pace while the others kept up with him. They tirelessly worked at reducing the gap between them and Gravelburn this way.

*   *   *

Gravelburn knew they would be out of the forest soon. He had noticed that the trees of the forest were starting to thin out, which could only mean one thing – they were approaching the boundaries.

'Maybe we should have waited and hid in the forest instead,' John suggested. 'That way, if Guardians then went past us, we could head off in a completely different direction.'

'And if they took their time coming to us, or headed for Rochg Infini instead, would we be squatting in the forest for all that time, or having a picnic, just waiting for them to turn up so we could go in a different direction to

19

them? Dumb idea, fleshing – except that you're not a fleshing anymore. You're a floatling.'

'Don't!' hissed John.

Soon the path opened out to a wide expanse of ground. Gravelburn carefully surveyed the area to make sure no one was in sight, but the only sign of life was the delightful chirping of birds, which suddenly stopped when Gravelburn and his companions stepped out into the open. Gravelburn then spotted the track he was looking for and they proceeded along it for a hundred paces until the track divided in two.

One way was rumoured to be very dangerous, and the other to be relatively safe. Gravelburn could not remember which was which, but if he and John were going to be travelling together, leaving the mini Rochgwar on his own, then in Gravelburn's evil mind it was obvious that Monty would go on the dangerous route so he and John could move swiftly without difficulty towards their objective.

'Us, this way. You, that way,' Gravelburn told Monty. It felt good giving orders again.

*   *   *

The Guardians were by now in the heart of the forest. But it was boring for all of them to keep counting fast and slow steps, so while Robin did the pacing, the others remembered to keep up, but also had a chat amongst themselves.

Someone started a conversation about which animal was the best, which quickly turned into a shouting match:

'Sharks!'

'Dogs!'

'Pigs!'

'I don't know!'

'Owls!'

'Bears!'

'Hawks!'

Robin was trying to keep count of the steps, but every now and then his focus was distracted at critical points.

'196, 197, 198, 199 ... '

'Whales!'

'100, 101, 102 ... 198, 199 ... '

' ... but not all owls are nocturnal! Some are diurnal!'

'100, 101 ...'

In this way, they ended up moving faster than they realised. But it also meant they were not pacing themselves, and were getting more tired than they realised. Taking a few hundred extra paces every now and then was fine. But doing it repeatedly would mean that they would pay for their exertions later. And it might be at a time when they could least afford it.

First Option

They had been walking for hours now. A moderate breeze wafted through the air. Then the breeze wafted some bees towards John, and they lingered around him because they thought he was a lovely pearl-white flower. John screamed. He didn't like bees so he flapped about, screaming. This made it even worse, because the bees were drawn to this pearl-white flower flapping its petals invitingly and they came even closer to get to the juicy nectar. Unfortunately, the bees just kept passing through John, smacking into each other. John flapped even more to get them away, when he realised they were not just near him, but within him.

All this time, Gravelburn was just looking at John like he was a complete lunatic.

'Stop shouting!' screamed Gravelburn. 'You'll draw attention!'

His voice echoed across the expanse. '*You'll draw attention – attention – attention!*'

The bees eventually left John alone and the two of them kept on walking. John was relieved that the bees had left, but Gravelburn was still fuming at him. They walked on in silence until they came to a cornfield. Rows of corn stood in neat straight lines, as far as the eye could see. Suddenly, Gravelburn saw the sun reflecting off something shiny. Could it be the glint of an axe?

Before he knew what was happening, he was wrestled to the floor and punched in the leg. John couldn't help, partly because he was a ghost, and partly because the bees had re-appeared and were bothering him again.

'We've goddim now, boys!' laughed a bandit. There were three other chuckles in reply. Gravelburn saw that they were trying to tie him up, so he spun on his back, kicked out at them, and then back-flipped to his knees and stood up. He dodged the blow of one charging bandit, grabbed him by the ankles and lifted him off his feet. The bandit hit the ground and Gravelburn spun him around into another bandit, like a hammer throw. The remaining two bandits were now rushing towards him. One held a knife and the other had an axe in his hands. Both looked threateningly at the rocky figure as they rushed forward.

The Rochgwar leader prepared himself as they charged. The axe passed over Gravelburn's head as he ducked, but he managed to grab the handle, kick the bandit and wrestle it out of his hands. Then he *thwacked* it into the other one.

The bandits fled. '*Gon ga gswar!*' shouted Gravelburn after them.

'Great work Gravelburn! Now could you ask these bees to go away?' requested John, still flapping about.

*　　*　　*

Power Unit finally emerged out of the forest. They briefly stopped arguing about animals amongst themselves, and were now actually talking about which way to proceed.

'We had this kind of discussion last time!' groaned Fil.

'If anyone is thinking about using blindfolds to randomly choose again, then no!' insisted Jack.

(On a previous occasion when they were faced with deciding how to pair up to enter a set of tunnels, they had blindfolded themselves and left it to chance to find a partner.)

'Guys! Guys!' said Robin. 'Stop it! I have a better idea. Why don't we look at the footprints? The footprints there?' He drawled on the last word for emphasis.

A short while later, the Guardians embarked on the same path as that taken by the minion. Heath, the commander of his own Messenger Unit, had somehow convinced the others the bigger set of footprints were a decoy.

Gravelburn and John had already faced a swarm of bees and four bandits. But the only obstacle for Monty was in choosing what to eat at the tavern he chanced upon.

*   *   *

Gravelburn and John were moving through a meadow when Gravelburn saw a little cottage. He kept it to himself and decided not to tell John about it. John would have asked to stop, but Gravelburn really wanted to press on and put as much ground as possible between him and any pursuing Guardians. But he had to admit that they had been moving for quite a while now and the lure of a rest was becoming quite irresistible.

Gravelburn crouched down. John was still playing with his bee buddies, which were eagerly buzzing around him, so Gravelburn flashed the famous Rochgwar family scowl.

'Whazzat for?' puzzled John.

The bees paused in flight, took one look at Gravelburn's face and they zoomed away. 'It wasn't for you,' Gravelburn explained. 'It was for the bees.'

After the brief rest, they carried on walking on in silence – well, at least Gravelburn did. John just hovered along over the ground. He suddenly noticed a small shape in the distance! He had spotted the cottage and smoke was rising from its chimney. It all seemed very welcoming and looked like it might be a nice place to go to.

'Look!' said John. 'A cottage!'

'Quick!' hissed Gravelburn, like he had suddenly remembered something. 'Take cover!'

They both crouched in the long grass. 'Why are we hiding?' asked John, puzzled.

'I've heard of Guardian outposts,' hissed Gravelburn. 'This could be one of them.'

'What do yo –'

'Shh!' uttered Gravelburn. 'They might hear us!'

After what seemed like two or more minutes, John asked, 'Are we going to move, or stay here and wait for someone to come and find us? Perhaps when we see them, we could move in the opposite direction?' Gravelburn paused for thought. The place might be worth investigating. He slowly inched forward on his elbows. The thorns scraped his armour and the grass tickled because it was   high up to his nose. He also dragged himself over some rabbit droppings – his senses of touch, smell and taste coming in handy here – and eventually got to the door of the cottage, where John was already waiting impatiently.

'What took you so long?' John, clean as a whistle, asked Gravelburn, who was all muddy, grassy and dirty.

They entered the house. Well, at least Gravelburn did – John just went through the door before Gravelburn opened it.

The inside reminded them more of a farmer's cottage. Strangely, it also had a mezzanine. There was a table and three chairs in the corner and some cupboards. Nobody was there but it was definitely inhabited, since there were all the essentials like water, food and a bed. There was also a half-eaten loaf of bread and some butter on the table. Gravelburn put his stone-cold hands (get it?) near the burning fire to keep warm. John tried to sit down on a chair but he kept falling through it, landing on the floor repeatedly. Gravelburn cursed him under his breath as he looked over his shoulder. 'Don't get comfy,' he ordered. 'We're leaving soon!'

As soon as Gravelburn's hands were reasonably warm, the two of them left. On his way out, Gravelburn picked up the loaf of bread. He hadn't really given much thought about why the fire had been burning. The door shut and two faces looked over the mezzanine.

Missed Opportunities

As they climbed down from the mezzanine, one asked, 'Was that John's voice we heard?'

'I don't know and I don't care,' grumbled the other. 'He took my bread!'

'The other one wasn't John,' said the first, whose name was Wistan. 'That was –'

(Duh-duh-DUH!) They both gasped, 'Gravelburn!'

'We need to contact somebody! Tell Murx Espin!' said Dulnas, the other. They were both Guardian scouts.

'But how?' wondered Wistan as a bay owl perched on a tree outside the cottage. They saw it through the window. The owl gave them a look that meant, 'I know! You want me to carry some message to some other fellow!' and rolled its eyes.

The two Guardians looked at it and grinned sheepishly.

Then they wrote out a message and rushed outside towards it.

The owl, whose name was Finn, took off with its message and instructions to deliver it. He soon encountered a brewing storm, and as he fought through it, he thought, 'It's the fault of that stupid eagle, Hunter! He's gone on holiday again!'

Finn was left with no choice but to continue on his mission. He faced strong headwinds which strongly resisted him. It had been drizzling but now rain was falling heavily from the sky. The thunder clapped loudly. Normally, he would have sought shelter in a tree until the storm passed, but he was desperate to deliver the message.

'I must do this! Delton depends on me!' He thought of the best messenger owls in his family line, and how they had battled greater obstacles to deliver messages that changed the course of history.

Finally Finn arrived at where Dulnas and Wistan had sent him. He was supposed to meet someone from

Delton at the point where the track split in two. Yet when he arrived, no one was there to be seen.

'Great, just great,' he thought. 'All that for nothing.'

*   *   *

Meanwhile, in the tavern, Gravelburn's minion was stuffed. Monty had eaten forty-two chicken nuggets, twenty-eight portions of fish and chips, thirty-five burgers and seventeen pepperoni pizzas.

For starters.

When he had walked in, Monty had said to the owner in old Rochgwarian, *'Mich stock en ngawshunts engula!'* which meant, 'I want everything you have!'

Unfortunately, the owner could not understand what he said. In the end, Monty just had to climb over the counter, make his way into the kitchen and grab whatever he could see. The owner had let him get on with it and have everything he wanted, thinking he would pay for it afterwards. After all, that was what happened in taverns, right? Eat first, pay later?

*   *   *

The Guardians walked on. They started to feel tired and hungry. This was because Nitro had picked up the scent of roasted lamb being cooked somewhere, so the Guardians had to hold him back from following his nose. They had also been marching for the better part of twelve hours, because they wanted to catch up with 'Gravelburn'.

Cut accidentally bumped into the back of Fil and was grumpily insulted. Then he stopped so abruptly that the Guardian behind, Heath, clattered into him.

To make things worse, they felt droplets falling from the sky.

'Oh, great!' announced Slick.

'The footprints end here,' said Ember.

'Well, we can all see that ourselves, Ember,' Robin grumbled.

'Robin!' called out Jack from the back. 'Should we stop?'

'No!' was the answer. 'We have to keep moving if we are to find and apprehend Gravelburn!'

'Could we at least stop by over there,' asked Fil, gesturing at a small tavern, 'and see if there is any space to take cover from this rain?'

'I can smell food,' said Fil. 'I think it could be baked potato rolls.'

'Baked potato rolls!' gasped Robin. He could hear the singing of angels in his head, going *'Ahhhhhhhhh'* as he thought of baked potato rolls … in a trance, he started to move towards the cafe, but quickly snapped out of it after three or four steps.

'No!' he cried out. 'We keep moving! There's not enough space for all of us there anyway.'

'Aw...' came the chorus of disappointed Guardian voices – even Ember's. They were all very hungry.

Inside the cafe, a small rocky figure watched the stream of Guardians march past, as he attempted to trade his collection of rocks to pay for the food he had just guzzled.

Friend or Foe?

Gravelburn and John felt like they were in a video game and had just received some health points. Well, actually only Gravelburn did, because whenever John tried to eat a piece of bread, it just fell through his body onto the ground and he giggled playfully. Although John kept trying to show Gravelburn his trick, the latter's initial response was always to flash him the Rochgwar family scowl. Gravelburn did, however, seem to be feeling better after his food had digested. Once, the sides of his mouth had flickered upwards. But only once, and only very briefly! For the rest of the time he trudged on grumpily, with John laughing merrily at his side.

Dulnas and Wistan were tracking the duo from a distance of about seventy paces behind.

'How is my bread passing through him?' wondered Dulnas in amazement.

'He's a ghost, you dummy!' replied Wistan, flustered, as he *clonked!* Dulnas on the head with the hilt of his sword. The sound of the sword bouncing off the head of Dulnas was very echoey – as if the latter's head was solid as wood.

'But if he's a ghost, how is he picking up the bread?' further wondered Dulnas.

'It's not really important for now. Just pay attention!' cried Wistan in frustration, and he *clonked!* Dulnas again.

'I *am* paying attention! I am trying to work it out!'

'I mean, pay attention and follow Gravelburn. Not pay attention to the bread!' *Clonk!*

Dulnas was not going to just stand there and take hits.

He *clonked!* Wistan in return with his mace, landing a blow right on his thigh.

'Owwwww – er!' protested Wistan, clutching the area in agony.

'Good things come in pairs!' continued Dulnas, with a blow to the other leg.

Wistan was now crouched in pain, yet springing up to try and somehow ease the pain in his legs. He looked just like a hopping frog. But it didn't stop him from trying to grab Dulnas in revenge. Dulnas kept trying to push him away. They tussled and each got some strikes in. After a while, they both looked like they had crawled through nettles while rocks had been thrown at them. They were not seriously hurt, but there were other important things they had forgotten about.

'We've argued so much that they've gone now!' said Wistan.

'Is it my fault?' replied Dulnas, his eyes wide open in amazement. 'You were the one distracting me, *Wuzztan*!'

'I dare you to say that again, *Dumbnas*!' retorted Wistan.

Dulnas threw a punch. In return, Wistan gave a kick.

Dulnas whacked him hard with a forearm, sending him backwards. Wistan threw a hand across the face of Dulnas, leaving a palm-sized print on the side. They wrestled and Wistan fell to the floor. Dulnas sat on him, squashing him like a blue whale on a grape. Despite this, Wistan somehow broke free, and body slammed Dulnas onto the ground.

'Oww!' said Dulnas. '*Allrightallrightallright!* You win – oww!'

'Yes!' Wistan said triumphantly, rising up and punching the air in delight.

One hundred paces ahead, Gravelburn and John heard squeals of pain and cries behind them. The bread slid through John for the umpteenth time but he was slow to pick it up. 'What was that?' he asked in a slightly worried tone.

'Must be wild animals,' Gravelburn concluded. 'Some of them could be dangerous. It might be better to go back to the cottage and hide there temporarily.'

So they flanked the area where they thought the screams had come from, and carefully retraced their way back to the cottage, making sure to avoid the dangerous animals they had heard (which were actually Dulnas and Wistan).

Pursuit

Meanwhile, Finn was pondering his next move. 'Hmm. I wonder what I should do …'

He looked around him. There were lots of trees behind him. He thought about having a rest in one of them, but he wanted to complete his mission first. As long as the message remained undelivered, whatever rest he had and however comfortable it was would be spoilt by the thought of the incomplete mission.

'I could go back to Del… actually no, the Guardians might return to this spot and it would be too late then,' he thought. 'Or I could follow where this other path goes, since I had come from the other.'

Finn stretched and prepared his wings. He had already figured out his plan of action, now all he needed to do was to execute it. The track split into two paths, and he had come down one of them. There was no one waiting, so he decided to go down the other – the one

43

taken by Monty, and also by Power Unit.

*   *   *

Dulnas was finishing dusting all the dirt and leaves of himself as Wistan scanned the area for Gravelburn and John. They both felt quite worried because they had lost track of their target.

'What shall we do?' asked Dulnas.

'I don't know,' said Wistan. 'No wait, I do! Let's have a picnic here! We'll set up a picnic blanket and lay out six plates – two for our dollies, two for us and two for Gravelburn and John. We'll have chicken drumsticks! We'll have mangoes! And nuts! And soup! And sausages! And cookies! And we'll get Fil to play the clarinet! I heard he's been learning the violin too, so maybe that as well! We'll have ten blue unicorn dancers! Magic shows! And we'll ask Gravelburn to come back to Delton with us and write his autobiography. It's going to be the best picnic ever!'

'Really?' said Dulnas in a hopeful voice. 'I love unicorn

dancers. They are my favourite.'

'No, you idiot!' Wistan delivered a blow to the head of Dulnas. 'We move forward and give chase!'

They dashed off, hoping to make up lost ground, and keeping their fingers crossed that Gravelburn was still ahead and within their range. But they didn't realise that while they were having their fight, Gravelburn and John had gone around them and back to their cottage.

Dulnas and Wistan, of course, were not the only ones in pursuit of the Rochgwar leader on the other track. Robin and the other Guardians were also hot on his heels – or so they thought, even though they were actually following Monty's tracks. But soon they were walking around cluelessly, because the tracks that they had followed had disappeared.

'Are you sure we're on the right path?' asked Cut.

'Duh!' exclaimed Fil. 'There's only one path, dummy!'
'You think you're so smart – where does this path lead to, and where does it end? Are we on a long circular

walk that will take us back to Delton in three months?' questioned Nitro.

'Hey everyone! Look! There are a load of footprints there. A whole group must have passed through here,' said Slick, pointing behind them.

'I spy ... something beginning with N,' Nitro announced, before pointing at Slick. 'It's 'no-brains'! Those are OUR tracks, for heaven's sake.'

'Are we going to –'

'BE QUIET EVERYONE!' Usually Robin was calm but he was completely going nuts now. Sometimes he regretted being a captain – this was one of those times. He recalled the occasion when Vei Sirage informed him that Murx Espin had promoted him to the rank of captain. This had happened when he was a mere eight years old – a captain at eight years old! He had felt very happy then and couldn't wait to go on his first mission in charge. Now he did not feel so much joy. He sometimes wished now that he wasn't in charge, because he hated having to make decisions, and also being questioned for his decisions.

'I think there's a base up ahead,' said Robin.

He paused for a while, trying to remember its name.

'Lacton,' he finally said.

'How do you know?' asked Fil.

'Because,' said Robin, much calmer than he had been a few minutes ago, 'I've memorised the Book of Delton. Lacton is mentioned in it. I think Gravelburn might be headed in that direction, but I'm not sure why. We're all getting tired and grumpy, so let's all take a two-hour rest. One of us will stand guard.'

'But that one person won't be able to take a rest!' protested Nitro. 'That person's definitely not going to be me.'

'Me neither!' Fil was quick to pipe up.

'Count me out! I've walked so far and for so long, my

feet might have fallen off somewhere back and I wouldn't know!' Jack squealed.

And so the cries of protest quickly rang out, until the only person left who had not cast his vote was Robin. Too late.

'Leadership by example, Captain Robin!' one of his 'friends' called out.

Robin sighed. There were some days where he absolutely hated being in charge.

Headed for Lacton

Gravelburn looked under the table. Gravelburn looked under the chairs. Gravelburn looked under the bed. 'There they are!' he cried triumphantly, as he pulled something out from under it. 'I remember them from last time!'

'Wow!' exclaimed John. 'They really suit you!' he said as someone vicious, someone dark, someone who didn't know the meaning of fear, stepped out from around the corner ... wearing bunny slippers.

'They squeak too!' said Gravelburn excitedly. He was definitely having a great time.

John was having a great time too. He hovered up on to the mezzanine level and found an old copy of a familiar book. 'I remember being made to memorise this book!' he said as he leafed through the pages.

Gravelburn walked up – *squeak squeak* – and snatched the Book of Delton from John. He flicked through the pages, and said in an annoyed voice, 'This is out of date! You see this base here?' he pointed to one of the pages.

'Yeah,' said John, 'it's called Lacton.'

'It was destroyed by the Rochgwars many solstices ago. The people there made crafts and weaponry, but this base was taken over by the Rochgwars soon at the start of the second Rochg-Lac war.'

'Really? Why do you know so much about it anyway?' puzzled John.

Gravelburn clasped the book shut, and took in a sharp deep breath before announcing to John, 'Because that's where were headed.'

He looked at John's face. John's mouth was wide open. He was either stunned with shock, or dumb with ignorance.

Gravelburn ignored the look on John's face – even though it was very distracting. The look on John's face was similar to a squirrel being told that nuts were poisonous. Gravelburn averted his eyes and continued.

'A long time ago, Lacton was a primary Guardian base. It produced explosives, weapons and armour. The Rochgwars realised that if we captured it, then not only would we stop Delton getting resources, but we could take the weapons for ourselves.

'Later, a huge assault began. I was only a foot soldier back then. Our ruthless commander Grontire ordered all units to storm the base, and we captured it while under fire from arrows and all the other weaponry Lacton produced. Only three of ten units survived the invasion.

'But a few moons after we had captured it, an army of Guardians attacked the base. Our army was already in a weakened state, and Grontire decided it would be better to blow up the base instead of letting the Guardians regain control. Everyone there perished in the explosion. Everyone ... except me.'

'How did you survive?' asked John. It seemed a bit strange that everyone except Gravelburn had perished.

Perhaps Gravelburn had hidden away in fright?

'Gravelburn is always ... one step ahead,' is all the Rochgwar would say.

John changed the topic. 'I'm supposed to have memorised the book of Delton a long time ago, but I don't recall Lacton. But why are we going there, if it has been abandoned for many years?'

Gravelburn walked down the steps to the ground level. *Squeak! Squeak! Squeak!* He grabbed a chair and proceeded to sit down by the fire.

'Rochgwar remnants transform back into Rochgwars, as you know from last time. I cannot fight the Guardians on my own. I need to find enough Rochgwars there to rebuild my army. The Guardians can only be defeated if there are enough Rochgwars to take them on. Maybe the Rochgwars that I think are there are awaiting a leader. A leader to free them. A leader who will take them to new heights of evil. Someone dark, someone vicious, someone who doesn't know the meaning of fear." Gravelburn paused to let John take in the full meaning of his words, and waited for his admiration.

'Cool!' replied John. 'And who might that be?'

'You're really lucky you can't feel anything,' huffed Gravelburn. 'You're fortunate you won't feel my fist passing through you.'

'Your head might be empty, but luckily for you ... Gravelburn is always one ... step ... ahead!'

*   *   *

Wistan and Dulnas were feeling very glum. They thought that they had lost Gravelburn and John. Both of them were up for yet another squabble, to blame the other for losing sight of the enemy. Except that they'd already had a couple of fights before, and those had not resulted in anything useful.

'What shall we do now?' asked Dulnas.

'Are there any nearby bases around?' wondered Wistan. 'We could ask them for help, or we could go back to Delton and at least tell Murx Espin that we know Gravelburn and John were on this path. You're the one who was supposed to know the Book of Delton inside out, not me.'

'Well ...' thought Dulnas.

After a while, he continued, 'Well ...'
It seemed like he was mentally flicking through the pages of the Book of Delton.

'Well ...'

'The Guardian base of Lacton is the next sign of civilisation from here,' he recalled. 'It's north-north-east from where we are right now,' he said, after he had consulted his prismatic sundial. So that is where they ended up heading.

Also headed for Lacton, on the other path to Dulnas and Wistan, were the eight members of Power Unit. Robin did not feel very good, and the songs led by Cut and Fil did not help. All the Guardians – except Robin – were feeling nicely rested and refreshed, and were

experiencing a high in energy. They sang as they
marched in step:

Boom! Boom! Boom!
The Rochgwars meet their doom!
Boom! Boom! Boom!
They'll get there very soon!

'It's really amazing how energised you can feel, and
what you can do, after you have had a bit of rest!' Jack
exclaimed over the commotion of:

You put your sword arm up
You put your shield arm down
You do the bashy-bashy and you turn around

'You must be cautious though!' shouted Ember.

'Says the person who's chucking his sword around!'
said Slick. Ember grinned sheepishly.

They were not far from Lacton now. Soon all this
trudging would be over, and they could relax for a little
while. The Delton Guardians could see the walls of

Lacton high atop the hill in the distance. And their hearts rose in the hope that the Guardians there would help them re-capture Gravelburn. The famed Power Unit would join forces with the Lacton Guardians, capture Gravelburn, and bring an end to all those attacks on Delton. They would capture him – wherever he was.

A Good Walk Spoiled

As Wistan and Dulnas rushed ahead on the first path, they could see what looked to them like a fort in the distance.

'That must be Lacton!' said Dulnas joyfully.

'Yes, but what's that coming towards us? They're big, they're burly, they're bonkers –'

(You guessed right! Rochgwars.)

'Quick! Into the bushes and don't move!' cried Wistan as a small patrol of Rochgwars rumbled past them. The two Guardians waited for a bit, in case more were following, but when they were confident the coast was clear, they both asked at the same time, 'How are there Rochgwars here?'

'I thought Rochgwars were wiped out by Captain Robin in the last battle!' said Wistan in disbelief.

'Rochgwars respawn from their remains; these ones must have done so,' Dulnas commented, rather wisely for a change.

'Whatever is going on here, it is something very, very strange,' said Wistan grimly. The two continued towards Lacton, but a little more cautiously.

Robin and the Guardians trudged on. For Robin right now, every step he took seemed to launch him one step further into a deep sleep that he had to fight against.

'Urggh. Nearly there, nearly there – *urgggggh*. When we get there Slick can take ch-*urgggggggh* of the troops and I can have a nice rest to rech-*urggggggggh* ...'

His legs felt like a Rochgwar had been strapped to each one, and that he was dragging them along.

In the Book of Delton, Lacton was described as a beautiful stronghold surrounded by lush green meadows. The Lacton Guardians were described as 'strong and industrious', and in addition to the armaments they produced, they also made traditional crafts such as scarves, perfumes and jewellery. The Ladies of Lacton choir often placed highly in traditional Guardian singing competitions, the book mentioned. Robin imagined that when his troops arrived at the gates, they would be warmly welcomed by the Lacton Guardians, and their Delton guests would be treated to a feast including wild boar, and most importantly, baked potato rolls!

Oh, how he loved baked potato rolls!

Robin wasn't expecting much, but in his current state he wondered if, inside Lacton, there might be a big statue of him as the Delton Guardian who helped defeat Gravelburn's Rochgwars and Flygwars, along with a placard describing how he was made a captain on his ninth birthday. Perhaps the Lacton Guardians had also turned to making collectible figurines of him and his friends. And perhaps their big welcoming feast might include baked potato rolls and sausages with the correct amount of meat and sweetness. And in addition to that, maybe also steak! And cookies! And drinks! Bacon! Sandwiches! Robin's friends were probably thinking the same thing, although each was imagining a statue of himself within the base.

Before they could get there though, there was still one final uphill walk.

It looked like it would take about five hundred paces to the top. Robin was sure it would take more. The reason Lacton was sited on top of a hill was so that it could overlook the ground below, which was great for its own security. But not so great for visitors.

Power Unit slowly made its way up the rocky path. The legs of the Guardians ached with every step. Soon, it seemed like they had no sensation in their toes. Lacton seemed to disappear into the mist that was starting to form. Their spirits were low, but they kept thinking of the delights of Lacton that they would get once they arrived.

Hoping to motivate his friends, Nitro cried out, 'I spy –'

'No!!!' Slick and a few others stopped him immediately.

'Think positive thoughts, guys!' encouraged Robin.

'Hmmph! There won't be any Rochgwars to bash here,' grumbled Fil.

'I'm going to pass out!' said Jack nervously.

'Just a few more steps guys!' Robin urged the Guardians on. They plodded on for the next hundred, dragging their weary feet. Slowly and surely, pace by pace, they covered the remaining ground. Everyone could see the walls of Lacton come into view – even the main door, with its sliding window and brass knocker slowly came into focus. Robin raced up to it with renewed energy and knocked excitedly, pleased to have arrived. *Tak-tak-tak-tak-tak!* He knocked and heard excited footsteps from inside; eager footsteps racing up to the door. Then the window slid open, and a cheerful voice spoke.

'Grast vi tuk?'

Here, There and Everywhere

Robin was very confused. He had been half-dreaming about having a rest and a delicious meal, but instead he got a reception from an ugly Rochgwar. Yes, it was smiling cheerfully, but it was still ugly. But Robin was not the only one that was confused.

'What are these strange beings, and what are they doing here?' thought the Rochgwar, who was obviously not accustomed to seeing humans.

Robin quickly slammed the sliding window shut from the outside.

'What shall we do?' panicked Jack.

'How about we charge in?' suggested Cut.

'That sounds dangerous, why not sneak in instead?' Ember piped up.

'Sneak in?' sneered Fil. 'That Rochgwar's already seen us, Ember. There's no point in being cautious.'

'None of those! Retreat!' shouted Robin in a somewhat dreamy state, as he heard a clang of metal from the other side of the door. 'Everybody run!'

'But we just walked up here!' a voice protested.

'We didn't trudge up all the way up this hill just for nothing!'

Suddenly, the door burst open to reveal rows of bloodthirsty Rochgwars waiting behind.

'Great idea, Robin!' said everyone. They had all been ready to challenge his last order, but now they charged downhill as fast as their legs could carry them. They had thought their legs would fall off as they first climbed up the hill, but it was surprising to them now what energy remained in them as they retreated. A hail of spears rained down on them. The Guardians were fortunate that the spears did not hit, because the Rochgwars had very bad aim and technique. Instead of flying straight through the air, in a spiral motion, the spears spun end over end, so they did not fly far.

A cry of *'Guta sim paar!'* echoed through the ranks of the stone monsters. Rochgwars wielding crossbows then rushed forward. They raised their crossbows to shoulder level and fired. These were more accurate than the spears.

'I spy with my –'

'Arrow!' said everyone else.

'How did you all know?' puzzled Nitro as one flew past him and embedded itself into a tree. The tail of the arrow shook violently on impact.

The Guardians had now escaped to the lower slopes to regroup. They were breathing heavily after their sprints.

'That was close!' gasped Heath.

'I wish we could have bashed them,' grumbled Cut.

'How did they get in there?' wondered Ember.

'Isn't Lacton supposed to be a Guardian base?' thought
Heath.

There were no quick answers for these questions. But
there wasn't time to think about answers in the first
place. So the Guardians focussed instead on what they
were going to do next.

'Should we go back to Delton?' asked Jack.

'You must be joking!' Slick gave him an evil look. 'In
case you haven't realised, we've come up all this way
from Delton!'

'Maybe we should move up the hill and take them out!'
suggested Fil.

'You must be joking!' Slick now gave Fil an evil look. 'In
case you haven't realised, we've just run down all this
way from Lacton!'

'Not now, not now,' Robin calmed his friends down, 'even though we will have to face the Rochgwars at some point.'

'Yes!' Cut celebrated excitedly, punching the air with his fist.

'Perhaps we should spread ourselves out into teams so the Rochgwars cannot concentrate their attack on us?' suggested Ember.

'Robin, you're in charge,' Slick reminded everyone. 'What is your plan?'

But Robin was fast asleep by now. He had sat on a rock, placed his head against a tree trunk and fallen asleep. It was a wonder to the others how someone could actually sleep sitting upright.

'I guess I'm in charge, then,' said Slick excitedly. 'I think we should –'

Suddenly, big rocks started falling from the sky.

'Gyro see gras ni!' a Rochgwar commander could be heard shouting.

'Aiyeet boges!' echoed his troops. Another salvo of rocks was launched up into the sky. The Rochgwar catapult commander, whose name was Gridie, watched the rocks fall and took note of where they landed. Gridie ordered his men to reload and fire.

'Duknir ad dee grassar!' he screamed.

'Wiyeet boges tu!' the Rochgwars replied.

The Guardians were shocked. Rocks rained down from the sky. Some fell in front of them. Some fell behind. Others to the left, and others to the right. A small one even clonked Fil on the head.

'You'll pay for that!' he shouted as he shook his fist at the Rochgwars further up.

On the top of the hill, Gridie was very pleased. His catapult teams had now bracketed the Guardians. He knew how to manipulate the direction and tension of the catapults for different ground targets, so whichever way they chose to run, he had a firing solution. They were trapped. Eritnorg, his commander, would surely make him second-in-command for his talents!

'Gevrundy!' another commander shouted. At the sound of this order, the Rochgwar foot soldiers advanced downhill, protected by the rocks fired from the catapults. They charged forward, in a messy formation, with nobody in line.

'Look out!' warned Nitro as another salvo of rocks fell from the sky ... but along with them fell something feathery. Jack caught it before it landed. It was Finn!

The Guardians were infuriated.

'Rochgwars launching owls?' fumed Cut. 'That's really cruel! I know they were mean, ugly, evil monsters, but this is taking it to a new low!'

'Yeah!' shouted Jack. 'I support the DSO – the Delton Society of Owls and I'm going to report this to them.

The DSO helps endangered owls to thrive and flourish, and this owl is endangered!'

'Yeah, it's a bay owl!' Slick pointed out.

'Did you know there are nearly forty-five species of owls?' asked Heath, 'and that they camouflage in their habitats?'

'It's not a very good time to be talking about owls, you know!' said Nitro. 'I ...'

'Rocks incoming!' a few others interrupted.

'We must shelter the owl so it doesn't get hit,' said (guess who?) Ember. They quickly placed the stunned owl alongside the sleeping Robin, then formed a circle around both, and raised their shields. Rocks continued to fall and sometimes clanged off the shields.
The Guardians withstood the aerial onslaught huddled together in a formation like the Roman tortoise. They remained in that position like they were waiting for a thunderstorm to pass. After a while, a voice piped up. 'I

think hawks launch would better than owls from a catapult, don't you?'

'No!' growled Cut. 'Cheetahs would launch the best.'

'Ahem,' Ember chipped in, 'I think sloths are the best. They are very slow and cautious.'

'No,' said Fil, 'cats would launch really well.'

'Yeah,' said Heath, 'but when they land, would they be 'feline' good? Get it? Cat? Feline?'

'Stop it!' Jack said from under the shields.

The onslaught of rocks had slowed now to a trickle. It looked as if the Rochgwars had given up.

'Uh, guys,' pointed out Nitro, 'take a look at that.' He indicated to the owl. A small piece of paper had been tied around Finn's leg.

'Careful!' warned Ember. 'It might be a trap.'

'For goodness sake Ember,' sighed Fil, 'this ... '

'I'm pretty sure this isn't a trap, Ember,' said Slick as he loosened the string securing the paper. 'It's only a piece of paper,' he reminded, casting a weary look at Ember.

'You could get a paper cut,' Ember retorted.

As Slick unfurled the paper, Robin woke up with a jerk.

'Where's the pencil sharpener?' he questioned dreamily. Then he saw the paper in Slick's hand and asked, 'Hey Slick, can I have a look at that?'

'It's addressed to you anyway,' Slick said as he handed it over.

The note read:

Captain Robin,
Gravelburn is ahead of us!

He looked up to check the reaction of the others.

'Wow,' said Slick. 'People must think you can't read, Robin. They're always sending you short messages.'

'Wait, wait, wait – what on earth?' raged Fil as he digested the contents of the message. 'Gravelburn? Ahead of us? In Lacton? There?' He pointed uphill.

'So Gravelburn has been staging this attack on us!' fumed Nitro.

'Let's push forward and attack him!' suggested Cut.

'We must be cautious; Gravelburn might have more Rochgwars inside the base.' (Guess who said that?)

'Let's do a sneak attack! After these rocks start falling, we'll go around the other side of the hill, and try and breach Lacton from the other side!' Heath piped up.

'Mi think dat gud ideya!' said a voice from behind them.

The Capture

Robin dropped the paper and spun around. Rochgwars were emerging all around them from the rock-littered ground.

'What?' exclaimed Jack. 'You were here all this time?'

'Uhh ... yeah?' said a particularly nasty-looking Rochgwar.

Jack unsheathed his sword, trembling as he did so while eyeing his adversary.

The Rochgwars moved forward and closed in. 'Defensive positions!' ordered Robin. The Guardians hastily organised themselves.

The Guardians thought there were only a few Rochgwars amongst them. They were wrong. Each time they fought one off, another re-emerged in its place. And they just kept on re-emerging, like an endless stream of stone monsters. Their defence did not hold out. The Guardians were captured and taken to Lacton.

As they were bound and marched uphill, Heath blurted out, 'We should ha –'

'Shuddit!' roared a Rochgwar. 'No talk!'

'As I was saying,' continued Heath to the others, ignoring the Rochgwar, 'we should have come up with a plan that would have ...'

'You want stretch mouth, you sing song!' demanded the stone monster.

Heath paused. Then he turned to his fellow Guardians. He looked weirdly at them, then back at the Rochgwar who had chided him. Then he took a deep breath, expanded his diaphgram and said in a trilly voice, 'As I was sayyyyy-ing ... la la la ... we should have come up ... with ... with ... la la la ... a plan, a plan, a plan!' He turned back to the Rochgwar. 'That one good enough for you?'

The Rochgwar exploded. *'Nuh sing Gar Deeyan song! Sing Rochgwar song! Song leihk dees:*

'At Rochg Infini, my birth ...' growled the Rochgwar.

'Also, of many moreeeee!' echoed the other Rochgwars.

'Me Rochgwar!'

'He Rochgwar!'

The Rochgwar voices then blended in a call-and-response fashion, and sometimes also in unison.

'And now, us rocks we must depaaaart!

For da dream dat we dream will come truuue!'

The Rochgwar song leader turned to face Heath. 'Your turn to sing. You get all that?'

Heath gasped. Then he replied in a voice that was unusually timid for him, 'Er … I only got the first couple of words. You know, the "at" bit ...'

A long scream of frustration could be heard across the land. Then a long silence fell over the trudge uphill – but not for long. Soon the Rochgwars were discussing whose singing was best.

"Lisen dis. Se gnaar ga fon ..."

"Dis better. Ahem. Nor, me no tak ..."

"Dis even more better. For Rochg Warus, for one ..."

Even though their hands were bound, the Guardians were trying to cover their ears from the din.

'The singing's terrible!' yelled Slick.
'Please, please, stop!' begged Jack.

The singing continued. *'Fi nar ca bo no!'* sang the Rochgwars.

'We're doomed!' squealed Robin.

Finally, they arrived back at the Lacton entrance. The Rochgwar singing stopped.

'We're saved!' celebrated Robin, pleased that the noise had died down. The Guardians' spirits lifted.

'Finally, it's stopped!' said Cut gratefully.

But their happiness would not last for long. They were hustled inside the base. And what a sight it was.

Where they may have earlier expected to find Lacton Guardians making scarves, dresses, swords and shields and armour, they instead saw grumpy Rochgwar faces glaring at them.

'You Guardian?' leered one as it approached them menacingly.

'Uhh ... yes?' said Fil.

'THEN WE TEAR YOU UP AND EAT YOU FOR BREAKFAST!'

'You doomed!' said another who had come up. 'Us heard about our friends at Delton. You pay. You pay! And then you pay some more!'

The Guardians were marched along inside a base that many of them had only read about.

'This is definitely not the Lacton mentioned in the book of Delton!' whispered Nitro. 'What Vei Sirage has been teaching us in our classes back at Delton is incorrect!'

'So I noticed,' complained Robin. He was now in grumpy Robin mode.

'I'm always doodling in my workbook in Vei Sirage's classes,' Heath piped up.

As they were shoved into the centre of the camp, Ember noticed something peculiar.

'Look! Unlike the old Rochgwar base with one pile of rocks in the corner, this base has four!'

'Wow, Ember!' exclaimed Cut in mock admiration.

'That's the first time I've not heard you say "we must be cautious" or "be careful" or something like that.'

'I don't say that all the time, you know,' protested Ember.

'Yes, you do,' chipped in Fil.

'No I don't! You'd better be careful, or I'll deal with you later!' shouted an enraged Ember.

'Quiet, you lot!' a voice shouted out as someone dark, someone vicious, someone who didn't know the meaning of fear, stepped out from the crowd.

The Accidental Poet
(and he didn't even know it)

One half of his face was cracked, worn and had an eye missing from its socket. The other half of his face looked normal, but it was clear that this Rochgwar had been through a lot. His body looked old and with many jagged edges, unlike the smoother surfaces of younger Rochgwars. It was not Gravelburn. It was Eritnorg, who was the leader of these Rochgwars that had taken over Lacton. As he made his way slowly towards the Guardians, the Rochgwars divided to form a path for him to proceed – a very wide path.

'So ... these are the Guardians that I heard eliminated Gravelburn's troops.'

'Yes!' answered Fil defiantly. 'And we're not afraid to show it! So don't even think about trying anything funny!'

'Um ... actually I am a bit nervous,' whispered Jack. 'Could you please try not to provoke him?'

'Quiet!' roared Eritnorg. 'Or I will make you quiet – quiet forever!' The cracks in his body seemed to glow with a sort of blueish colour.

Eritnorg walked back and forth, peering intently at the Guardians. The look on his face was like an alligator who'd had his lunch stolen by a turtle, and who was now thinking of swallowing the whole turtle. The Guardians felt like the turtle being chased – basically, they were bound, incapable of moving fast, and trapped in enemy territory. They were also very, very tired. Robin was thinking of dozing off again. It was not a good place at all to be.

'I remember when I was once captured by Guardians,' growled Eritnorg. 'The children used me as target practice and threw eggs at me.'

'Hee hee,' giggled a few listening Rochgwars.

'I felt humiliated,' continued Eritnorg. 'Everyone laughed at me. Even the children did. I remember the feeling of disgrace. Egg yolk dribbling down my face. I wanted to get out of that place –'

81

'You're a poet!' gasped Nitro, as many Rochgwars nodded in agreement. *Uhh-huuuh.*

Eritnorg's face was red hot, which was rare for a Rochgwar, as they are usually stone cold. 'Stop looking at me like that, each mouth wide open like a hungry rat!' he ordered.

The Rochgwars were stunned.

'It's true!' said Fil, breaking the silence. 'You are a poet!' Some of the Rochgwars nodded in agreement, some applauded, while others burst out laughing.

Eritnorg ignored the reaction of the crowd.

'I may do it from time to time, but I certainly do not always rhyme,' he growled. The Rochgwars looked at one another. So did the Guardians.

'I'm starting to fill up with hate,' declared Eritnorg. 'I'll make you all pay later, just you wait!'

The Guardians and the Rochgwars burst out laughing.

Ember covered his mouth with his bound hands, but the rest of his body was shaking violently. One Rochgwar was furiously scribbling down Eritnorg's words for a future poetry book.

'If you all keep roaring with laughter, I'll make sure you pay for this after!'

Cut laughed so hard that he broke wind. 'Him have trouser tuba!' laughed a Rochgwar, pointing at the source. (Well actually, at the *bottom* of the source.)

The situation was turning to farce. Eritnorg was furious.

'Silence!' he bellowed. 'When I was used for target practice, it felt horrible. Now I will do the same with you.

'I didn't do it there, did I? Didn't rhyme, did I? Huh? Huh?" Eritnorg fumed arrogantly. The Rochgwar scribe looked up from his notes, disappointed.

'I will make sure you all suffer,' Eritnorg told the Guardians. '*You* will have egg yolk dribbling down your face! *You* will know the feeling of disgrace! You may think I'm lying, but I'm not trying to be rhyming!'

The Rochgwar scribe's face lit up at once, and he hastily started working his pen again.

Surprise Visitors

The Rochgwars were delighted. It was going to be fun! It was the first time in years they could throw eggs at humans. For some of the younger Rochgwars, it was going to be the first time they were dealing with human targets, so they were very pleased with what Eritnorg had decreed.

'Me want splat red cluck cluck egg on dat boy,' one Rochgwar pointed out the other next to him, as the cries of 'Eritnorg! Eritnorg! Eritnorg!' went up and the Rochgwars rubbed their hands in glee. The whole complex rang out with their cries of praise for the clever and thoughtful leader.

However, the Guardians were very indignant. 'I thought we were going to get a worse punishment!' said Heath. 'Come on! We are Power Unit, after all! Not just your average nobody!'

'You can be target practice for the catapult,' said Eritnorg, 'but I warn you – when it fires, with fear you'll gulp!'

The Rochgwars cheered for their leader. It was not sure if they were applauding his decision, or his poetry.

'Catapult practice?' pondered Gridie, the Rochgwar catapult commander. 'Woo hoo!' he growled in delight, punching the air before suddenly stopping. 'Shame only eight targets, need more. Need more!'

'Need more! Need more! Need more!' the Rochgwars chanted, working themselves up into a frenzy, as Power Unit were marched away to be imprisoned.

Outside Lacton, two figures trudged up the hill to the sound of muffled but excited voices. 'What do you think all that cheering is for?' puzzled one.

The other replied, 'Well, Gravelburn may think he have given us the slip earlier on, but there's no mistaking that sound. It means the Lacton Guardians have captured Gravelburn. Let's not miss out on the celebration!'

Dulnas and Wistan rushed up the hill. 'Do you think we

should knock?' asked Dulnas as he approached the door. 'Or should we proceed cautiously?'

'You're turning into the new Ember, Dulnas,' sneered Wistan. 'Of course we'll just go up and knock! It's the Lacton Guardians that live here!' He *thumped-thumped-thumped* the brass knocker furiously, like an over-excited woodpecker. Before anyone inside could say 'Gras vi tuk?', Wistan announced, 'We're Delton Guardians! We want to join in! Let us in quick! We don't want to miss out!'

The door opened. Dulnas and Wistan found themselves captured by laughing Rochgwars, and frogmarched along.

One Rochgwar, whose name was Gratin, said to his friend, '*Me wuz dreaming about more targit practise, and dey came!*'

His friend was astounded by how things had turned out. '*Dream some again! Dream some more!*'

'*Me do dat!*' Gratin decided as he pushed Dulnas and

Wistan onwards. They laughed at the silly Guardians that had just shown up, asking to be made targets. The other Rochgwars that they passed also leered at the Guardians. When the pair were brought to the middle of a great crowd of Rochgwars, they had an argument again, as they often did, about whose fault it was.

'You should have bought the new Book of Delton!' said Wistan angrily.

'It cost five Deltcoins!' protested Dulnas. 'So I just borrowed a copy from my grand-dad!'

'That copy's ancient!' retorted Wistan. 'The section on Lacton is outdated! Look around you!'

'So?' shouted back Dulnas. 'Are you trying to say my grand-dad's ancient?'

'It's not right!'

'I definitely agree! It's not right to make such comments about my grand-dad!'

'I mean,' said Wistan, stretching out his words, so that Dulnas could grasp his logic, 'The section on Lacton is not right! Where are all the blacksmiths? The famous craftsmen? The dancers? All we have is just a bunch of ugly rock fellas! All because you were too stingy to spend five Deltcoins!' Wistan was furious and his voice was cracking with anger. Dulnas was also raising his voice, as all around them, the ring of Rochgwars was goading them and chanting 'Fight! Fight! Fight! Fight!'

Dulnas looked around in amazement on hearing the sound of Rochgwars cheering him on. While he was distracted, Wistan balled up his fists and *wham!* A black mark on Dulnas's face popped up and grew in size. The hit stunned Dulnas, making him furious and he retaliated.

Dulnas threw a punch which caught Wistan in the forehead. 'Uff!' he cried, feeling like a boulder had just rolled down a slope and crashed against his brain.

'Come on!' cheered half of the Rochgwars. 'Good shot!'

'Thanks!' replied Dulnas, grateful for the attention, just

89

before a boot caught him in the mid-section and temporarily winded him.

'Aw ...' went the Rochgwars, disappointed that the fighter they had chosen to support had been hit. However, the other half, who were rooting for Wistan, cheered.

'Maybe next time do a rugby tackle!' suggested one Wistan supporter.

'Or stick yer finger in his ear and twist!' offered another.

Wistan did what the first Rochgwar had suggested. But as Dulnas stumbled backwards from the impact, his right leg wedged between himself and Wistan, and as they both fell, the right foot of Dulnas was lined up with Wistan's chest. He couldn't miss.

'Ooof!' cried Wistan.

'STOPPPPPPP!' the loud screeching voice of Eritnorg bellowed. The two Guardians, winded from their efforts, looked quizzically at each other and around themselves.

'Nooooo!' the Rochgwars begged the two Guardians.

'*Please no stop! Kerry on bish-bash-bosh! Fight! Fight! Fight!*'

Eritnorg flung aside the Rochgwars in his path as he made his way to the middle. He turned to look at the crowd. 'Do you want our targets to waste themselves? If you let them fight among themselves, there will be fewer targets for you!'

The Rochgwars turned and looked at one another. Soon one nodded his head, and then another joined in, and as more and more nodded their heads in agreement with Eritnorg, they broke out into a chant, 'No fight! No fight! No fight!'

Wistan and Dulnas held back their punches.

Eritnorg turned to face his Rochgwars. 'That's right, do we want to have more Guardians as targets, or less?'

'More! More! More!' the Rochgwars chanted. 'More! More! More!'

More? They wanted more? Dulnas and Wistan resumed trading punches.

'No fight! No fight!' shrieked the Rochgwars, anxious to save the two for target practice.

Dulnas and Wistan sighed in exasperation. 'Come on now!' they cried. 'Do you want us to fight, or not?'

Eritnorg had had enough. 'Stop this nonsense! Just take them to the Kaje!'

Infighting

At the far side of Lacton, opposite the entrance, was a section the Rochgwars called the Kaje. It was known as that because there was a big cage that they used to keep prisoners. Its current tenants were the Power Unit. Robin was fast asleep in the cold and dirty cage, while the others were discussing the situation amongst themselves.

'It's cold and dark in here ... wait, is that a human skull?' said Jack, pointing to a white object on the ground that he had just noticed.

'No, it's a rat's skull, you dummy,' said Fil. 'Or maybe it could be Cut's skull; the size is a bit similar.' Cut glared at Fil.

'It's still quite frightening!' worried Jack.

'Baby!' sneered Fil.

'Be careful,' warned Ember, 'there could be hidden traps around this cage. Don't move around unnecessarily.'

'Speaking of traps, I think we should make our own, don't you?' mused Heath. 'So that if any of the Rochgwars come back, we could slow them down, or trick them.' He removed his bootlaces, tied them together at one end, then tied the two free ends on the first two bars of the cage beyond the door. The end result was just about long enough. If the Guardians were all asleep and the Rochgwars came into the cage, the bootlace might trip them up, and distract them and give some sort of warning to the Guardians.

'Well,' mentioned Slick, 'Robin has fallen asleep – again – so in the absence of the leader, I guess I'm next in charge! I'm in charge – *woohoo*! I need to think of a plan!'

'We don't need a plan when we're here,' said Cut. 'We just punch everything we see!' One of the things Cut hated most was discussion.

94

'Hey guys, I spy with my little eye, something beginning with …'

But Nitro didn't get to finish what he was saying. Two burly Rochgwars marched towards the cage, unlocked it and shoved two new additions inside. 'Here come your rescuers!' they taunted as Dulnas and Wistan were forced in. Dulnas tripped over the bootlace trap Heath had set and fell face first to the ground the moment he crossed the threshold.

The Guardians felt slightly depressed when they saw that more of their number had been caught. 'Great rescue work, guys,' sighed Slick.

Dulnas and Wistan got to their feet. Wistan was re-acquainting himself with the Power Unit commanders, whom he had not seen for a long time, but Dulnas was now chasing Heath around the cage for revenge. The Guardians noticed that Wistan and Dulnas were not in a good state. They both had bumps on their heads, but Dulnas looked to have suffered more – he had several more cuts and scratches. How the Rochgwars must have tortured them! The Power Unit commanders felt for Dulnas and Wistan. Little did they know that the injuries the two had suffered were inflicted by each other during their previous tussles!

Inside the cage, Heath was trying to escape from Dulnas. 'Get away from me, you lunatic!' he shouted loudly.

Dulnas was like a raging bull to the red flag that was Heath, and he was pursuing him because he had tripped over Heath's trap. Before he had been sent to be a scout, Dulnas had been based in Delton and had endured many of Heath's pranks, including exploding bread and itchy feet powder. When he had tripped up entering the cage, Dulnas knew instantly whose fault it was and all the angry feelings in the past that he had held towards Heath rose up again inside him. The two went round and round inside the cage until Heath tripped over his boots, which had slowly been loosening themselves from his feet because they had no laces. He fell to the ground. Dulnas was about to deliver a punch to Heath when something held him back. Somebody was grabbing his fist and preventing him from striking Heath.

'Don't hit him!' warned Fil. 'He's a Power Unit commander. Respect!'

'Respect?' questioned the furious Dulnas, turning to face Fil. 'Respect my fist!' he yelled as he landed a blow on Fil instead. If Fil was preventing him from striking Heath, he would offer him the punch intended for Heath.

Cut then intervened with a punch that landed on Dulnas, hitting him between the eyebrows. The area swelled and it now looked like Dulnas's eyebrows had joined to become a single long line ... a bit like what Heath had done with his bootlaces.

'Oof!' groaned Dulnas falling backwards and growing even more infuriated.

Heath cried out, 'Don't do it, Dulnas! They're both Power Unit commanders. Resp –'

Thunk! Heath's mouth was now shaped like a fish as his head rolled to one side. The fight was on. For Dulnas, this was the first fight he'd had that did not involve Wistan. Wistan was just minding his business, talking to Slick and Ember.

'How's it going?'

'Not too bad. How about you?'

'Yeah, I'm alright. Fine thanks.'

'Why did you send us a message telling us Gravelburn was here?' asked Slick.

'I didn't,' clarified Wistan. 'Dulnas and I thought you would were behind us!' cried Wistan. 'When I wrote the message that Gravelburn was ahead, I sent the owl to where the track splits, so you would know which path to take. Did you not see him there?'

'I knew it!' Ember burst out emphatically, getting up to his feet and stamping the ground in frustration. 'I knew it! The owl! The message! We should have been more cautious! You guys keep imitating me behind my back – "you must be cautious, you must be cautious" – don't think I don't know it, but maybe now you see there's a reason for all that! I was right to be cautious!'

It was no good trying to waste time explaining the events that had led up to the present time. They were stuck in a cage in enemy territory with no means of escape. And they were all starting to get hungry again. And Robin – Captain Robin – was suffering from exhaustion and fast asleep.

'It's not looking good for us,' cried Jack, petrified. 'What do you think the Rochgwars want with us?'

'I spy trouble,' Nitro said. 'No wait! I should have just told you the opening letter, but instead I just gave you the answer!' he exclaimed, slapping his forehead at his own mistake. 'Even my I-Spy questions are failing! This is not looking good!' worried Nitro.

'Yeah,' agreed Slick. 'It's definitely not looking good if you are losing your touch when you're playing 'I-Spy'.' But he turned around and cupped his mouth with his hands, giggling secretly in celebration and not having to play I-Spy for the time being.

*   *   *

That evening, Eritnorg called a meeting with the other
Rochgwar commanders, including Gridie, Gronun and
Gronty.

'What do you think we should do with the Guardians?'
he asked.

'Ooh! Ooh! I know!' shouted Gratin, the Rochgwar who
had dreamt about having more targets.

'Yes, Gratin?' Eritnorg asked.

'How about we keep them at the Kaje, make them learn
Rochgwar songs, then make them sing Rochgwar
songs for everybody. If they forget the words, we throw
things at them!' suggested Gratin.

'*Grahahahahahaha!*' squealed the Rochgwars with a
mixture of laughter and excitement. They were
delighted at the thought of humiliating the Guardians
who had so often humiliated them in battle.

100

'Good idea!' said Eritnorg. 'But I have one thing to add to all that, Gratin.'

'Whatisit whatisit?' asked Gratin excitedly. *A reward for me?*

'How about ... we make them sing our Rochgwar songs in public, and whether they forget their words or not, we still throw eggs at them after that!' laughed Eritnorg.

'Good plan!' said Gratin, less excitedly. (What else could a lackey say to his leader?)

'As a reward, Gratin,' announced Eritnorg, 'you will be promoted!'

Gratin looked delighted. *'General Gratin?'* he wondered. It had a nice alliteration to it. He would be higher up in the command chain, ordering more Rochgwars about. All that for just coming up with a brilliant idea!

Gridie, who had commanded the catapults and helped in the capture of the Guardians, looked visibly disappointed. The look on his face seemed to say,

'What else do I need to be doing in order to get the praise I deserve from our dear leader Eritnorg?'

Knock knock knock! The meeting was suddenly interrupted at the entrance to Lacton.

'Ooh, more Guardians!' said Gratin, rubbing his hands with delight. 'You there!' he called out, pointing to a random Rochgwar. Eritnorg had just promised to promote him. He could start bossing others about.

The Rochgwar snapped to attention. 'Go open the door!' Gratin ordered.

The selected Rochgwar rushed up to the main door. He didn't seem very happy to be bossed about, but it was better to be bossed about and complaining, than to be a mute pile of rubble, so he did as he was told. He slid open the latch immediately without checking to see who it was. On the other side of the door, a hand pushed against it, and it was shoved forward with maximum power. The door flew open like a kite caught by a gust of wind, and the Rochgwar behind it was pushed

102

backwards and crumbled between the door and the wall.

'Here's Gravelburn!' roared a voice.

'And John!' squeaked someone else.

Guess Who?

Gravelburn looked around. He saw lots and lots of Rochgwars. He was very impressed by what he saw.

'Those Rochgwars will be great for my army!' he thought. 'They look strong. These ones here plus the ones trapped in the cave ... I might be able to take over Delton now!' He was very, very pleased.

But the Rochgwars at Lacton were definitely not pleased at all. They glared at this newcomer and thought, 'Who is this passing stranger who swaggers in like he is in charge here?' Every Rochgwar in the camp grabbed his weapon. Even the commanders at the table rose to their full height, eyeing Gravelburn's every move, and readied themselves. All except Eritnorg.

Gravelburn looked at the Rochgwars standing to attention, with their weapons drawn. A sustained smile appeared on his face – a very rare sight. In fact, no Rochgwar had remembered anything more than a flicker of a smile from Gravelburn. He thought proudly,

'Ah! These Rochgwars are paying respect to their leader – the one who has come and will lead them to victory against the pesky Delton Guardians!'

He decided to address the troops and headed for the table, from where he could stand and make his speech. From there, he could command his audience with a rousing speech that would end up with every single one chanting his name, ready to follow him to battle with the Guardians. He would be the one to spearhead the Rochgwar domination of the world! With every step he took, though, there was a unmistakeable sound. *Squeak! Squeak! Squeak!* He was still wearing the bunny slippers he had stolen from Dulnas.

The Rochgwars were puzzled by the slipper-wearing Gravelburn. They were also confused by John. 'What is that weird floaty thing?' they thought. One of them thought John was a strange flying stingray. Another thought he was a transparent eagle. The Rochgwars were all puzzled because they could see John, but they could also see through him, and he talked, and he could hover. What was this strange thing? And who was this Rochgwar who commanded this magic creature?

Squeak! With every step that Gravelburn took, the resistance from the angry Rochgwars diminished. As he approached, each and every nearby Rochgwar gradually lowered their weapons and their mouths gaped with shock. It was as if they were watching a magic trick, and could not figure out how Gravelburn was doing it. Gravelburn, in their eyes, might as well have been making cards disappear, or sawing himself in half.

The Rochgwars whispered urgently to each other, 'It's true! It's true! The prophecy has come true! The prophecy says, *'Beware the one who has squeaky feet, and commands the white spirit!'* The prophecy has come true! This is the Chosen One!' They fell to their knees and laid their weapons down beside them.

John floated alongside Gravelburn and said nervously, 'I could be wrong, but these guys look like they think you are some sort of god.'

'Ooooh,' said Gravelburn smugly. Then his manner suddenly changed, and he hissed to John under his breath, 'That sounds good ... but keep moving.' Still, it was difficult to strut when you have bunny slippers on and they make an embarrassing squeaking noise.

At the table that Gravelburn was soon approaching, Eritnorg winced and put his head in his hands. He could not believe what he was seeing. Even his own commanders at the table were kneeling on the ground, paying homage to this Rochgwar who had randomly popped up. Eritnorg hissed to himself, 'That prophecy is fake! I should have invented a crazier one!'

He jumped on the table and screeched in a whiny, high-pitched, know-it-all voice, 'Rochgwars! Actually – the prophecy says, "*Beware the one who has squeaky feet, commands the white spirit,* and brings his son. *Until then, Eritnog is Boss and all Rochgwars listen to him.*" That's what the prophecy actually says!'

'Uh?!' said the Rochgwars, still kneeling and thinking it over.

'That Rochgwar has squeaky feet ... but he has no son! He's not the Chosen One! He's not the Chosen One, and I'm the boss. You all only take orders from me!

Now don't just kneel there! Get up!'

The Rochgwars quickly rose to their feet and brandished their weapons again at Gravelburn. He was surrounded. There was no way he was going to fight his way out of this one. John watched the Rochgwars close in.

'This might get ugly,' Gravelburn said in a monotone.

'It can't get any worse for me,' said John cheerfully. 'I died in the last book! I'll be fine! Hee hee hee!'

For a moment, there was silence as everyone stared each other down, wondering who would make the first move that would lead to an all-out fight. The silence was broken by a pitter-patter of feet, as a little figure, in an unfamiliar sea of Rochgwars, headed for the only figures he knew.

'Monty!' cried John eagerly. 'Where have you been?'

Monty burped. After all, he had eaten a lot – a lot – of food. He had taken his time getting there. But he had arrived at Lacton at just the right moment.

The Rochgwars gasped. 'The prophecy is true! Squeaky feet – white spirit – son ...'

They laid down their weapons and knelt down once more to worship the Chosen One.

'All hail Gravelburn, the Chosen One! All hail Gravelburn, the Chosen One!' they chanted.

But those who had not heard Gravelburn's name clearly when he first entered the camp chanted, 'All hail Gravybun, the tasty one!'

Eritnorg sighed and rolled his eyebrows. 'Maybe I should have told them the prophecy says the Chosen One would come with teapots full of juice, balanced on top of upside-down elephants!'

Gravelburn was seriously pleased with this reception. He could get used to this. Then he noticed that someone wasn't kneeling. What a lack of respect! He squeak-marched his way right up to that Rochgwar and pointed a finger at him.

'You there! Respect your Chosen One!' Gravelburn was keen to take advantage of the Rochgwars while he could.

The figure looked at the finger. Then he dropped his eyes to the bunny slippers. Then he looked at John. Then Monty. He put his hands to his hips. Finally he allowed his eyes to rest on Gravelburn. And he laughed.

'So,' said Eritnorg eventually, 'it is you. The rumours I have heard are true. They say Gravelburn escaped from Delton after he was captured.

'I also heard he was hoping to gather more Rochgwars, after his own were destroyed by the Guardians.'

Eritnorg and Gravelburn locked eyes.

'I heard he was coming to lead us into battle, under *his* command.' Eritnorg paused at this, letting the words sink in, as if to say to Gravelburn, 'I will never *ever* be under your command.'

'And look who is here now! Who would have thought the lowly Rochgwar lieutenant would grow up to be Gravelburn, the Chosen One? *Ahahahahaha!'*

Eritnorg roared with laughter, as if to say, 'I can't believe this is happening! Gravelburn? The Chosen One?'

Then the laughter stopped abruptly, like a lit match that had been abruptly blown out.

'I thought you were the worst of my soldiers. It appears I might have been slightly wrong. You're not the worst. But you are definitely no Chosen One!'

Gravelburn's mind flew back over the lands of time, to a period when he was just a lowly soldier. Something about Eritnorg's words had kindled a distant memory. He carefully thought it over. He remembered the time when he was a junior lieutenant in the Rochgwar army, and who his commander had been. A thought struck him suddenly, like a lit match. He walked forward and

111

examined the face in front of him. He studied it carefully, then realised he could remember it vaguely from the past.

'I know your face. Your ugly, demented face. I know I've seen it before. I don't know your name. But that's just as well. I won't need to. You're the one who needs to know mine. Not the other way around.'

Eritnorg sneered and roared with maniacal laughter. 'You don't know my name? You don't know? *Arghaha!* Spell my name backwards and see what you get!'

'Ermm ...' grumbled Gravelburn. He hated to do any mental puzzles.

'*Emanym*?' offered John kindly. Monty giggled.

Eritnorg clenched his fists. 'No! Don't spell "my name" backwards, spell my name backwards!'

Gravelburn was smiling again at the sight of an infuriated Eritnorg. There was nothing more satisfying than seeing an adversary truly flustered by imbeciles.

John was hard at work again. 'I've got it! *Sdrawkcab Emanym! Sdrawkcab Emanym!* If I'm being honest, that's a rather silly name, not just for any leader, but for anyone, really. "Sdrawkcab" really sounds like a name you give to a parrot, or a sound that a crow makes. Who would want to be called that? But Gravelburn,' said John, turning his attention to his friend, 'I must say that this Rochgwarian language is so *bee-yoo-ti-ful!* I wanted to learn to speak it but you've not really had time to teach it to me yet. Could we find some time for you to teach it to me? Please? Please?

'I love the sound of it. The verbs, the nouns, the consonants, the alliteration, the way it rolls of your tongu –'

Gravelburn was annoyed at the sight of a dreamy, unfocused John. So he relented.

'Okay! Okay! Here's your first phrase to learn: *grush niem.*' Gravelburn hoped that this would be the end of John's incessant nagging.

'Ooh,' said John, excited to start on Rochgwarian for

113

beginners. '*Grush niem. Grush niem.* Did I get it right? *GRUSH NIEEEEM! GRUSH NIEEEEM!* But what does it mean?'

'It means "I have a small brain",' sniggered Gravelburn.

John felt cheated but excited to at least learn some Rochgwarian. The kneeling Rochgwars guffawed. Some toppled to the ground. Eritnorg watched the Rochgwars descend into heaps of chaotic laughter at the sight of the floaty spirit. The seriousness of the moment, when he would reveal the truth to all, had been spoilt.

'My name!' shouted Eritnorg over the din. 'My name – is Eritnorg! Spell. It. Backwards!'

Gravelburn looked at John for help. John would know the answer. Gravelburn was just lazy and thought that the Chosen One should not have to do the work, but John was too busy flying around the base, from wall to wall, showing off his new Rochgwarian language skills to anyone who would listen, and asking every other Rochgwar if his pronunciation was accurate or not, and if they could understand him. They sarcastically applauded and whooped.

So it was down to Gravelburn to do the hard work himself. 'Er ... Eritnorg ... G. Hmm... R. Gimme a sec ... O ...'

This continued for a while – too long, in Eritnorg's opinion. 'Are you done yet?' he growled. He had lost patience.

'You made me lose track!' roared Gravelburn in frustration. 'Now I'll have to start all over again!' And so he did ... and this time he worked it out, despite the distractions around him. He compared his answer with the face in front of him. The face actually looked older to how he remembered it, but there was undoubtedly a resemblance. This was Grontire, his former commander. The one who had tried to send him and other Rochgwars to destruction.

'I remember you now. So there, Grontire. Now respawned and reformed,' said Gravelburn as he walked back and forth an imaginary line on the ground.

John had returned to his side and Gravelburn now had the eyes and minds of the Rochgwars, who were still kneeling.

'I remember him!' he shouted to them, pointing an accusing finger at Eritnorg. 'He used to be my cruel commander from a long time ago. He made me climb up Rochg Infini carrying two Rochgwars on my back. He also made me smash my best friend into pieces.' Upon hearing this, Gratin's ears pricked up at the memory and he flashed a quick glance at Gravelburn, and then Eritnorg.

Gravelburn continued. 'And my cruel, cruel former commander here also –'

'Made you run around singing '*Grush niem*' to everyone!' interrupted Gratin.

Eritnorg laughed at the memories, with a devilish sort of tone, and also sniggered with delight now that his secret past identity had been unmasked. It was almost as if he was relieved now that he didn't have to pretend anymore about who he really was.

He addressed the crowd. 'I also remember the time I made these two,' he pointed at Gravelburn and Gratin, 'face each other and take turns throwing eggs at each other. It was so funny!'

Gravelburn seethed with rage. 'I had forgotten that embarrassing memory!'

He turned to the crowd and jabbed his finger repeatedly in Eritnorg's direction. 'This Rochgwar ... is the worst Rochgwar commander you will know. He tortures for fun. He is cruel, he is evil ...'

Gravelburn had meant to discredit Eritnorg's leadership, but a cruel and evil leader who tortured for amusement was actually – for Rochgwars – their idea of a great leader.

They all rose to their feet and looked at Gravelburn. Then one of them asked the question they were all thinking.

'Wait!' asked the Rochgwar. He looked at Gravelburn and puzzled, 'He commanded you?'

117

Then he looked at Eritnorg and posed the same question. 'You commanded the Chosen One? Wouldn't that make you higher up in command ... in charge of the Chosen One ... which means you are better than ...'

The Rochgwars debated over this new information. Eritnorg seized his chance. 'Yes! I commanded him! And the prophecy actually says, "*Beware the one who has squeaky feet ... blah blah blah ... blah blah blah ... and the Chosen One's commander is the real Chosen One!*" That's what it really, really, says!'

The Rochgwars fell to their knees yet again, but this time in front of Eritnorg.

'All hail Eritnorg! The Chosen One's Chosen One! All hail Eritnorg! The Chosen One's Chosen One!'

A Brief History of Time

Dear reader, you might be a bit confused at this stage.
You might be wondering, 'Where are the Guardians?' or
'Where is Finn?' Or perhaps you might be thinking,
'How is this all going to tie in together?' or 'How will the
Guardians escape?'

Above all, you may have already lost track and been a
bit confused by what is happening. So here's a quick
summary!

Gravelburn had escaped from Delton, with the
Guardians in hot pursuit. When the path divided,
Gravelburn and John went one way, while sending
Monty on the other path to mislead the Guardians. On
the left track that Gravelburn and John were on, they
were followed by Dulnas and Wistan, but Gravelburn
and John looped around the duo to return to their
cottage. Unfortunately, it was at this point that Dulnas
and Wistan dispatched Finn the owl to Robin with the
message, 'Gravelburn is ahead of us', meaning Dulnas
and Wistan thought that Gravelburn was ahead of them

119

on the first track.

Finn was supposed to meet the Guardians at the fork in the road, but could not find them there as they had raced ahead on the second path in pursuit of who they thought was Gravelburn, but unbeknownst to them, they were actually following Monty. But Monty had stopped to eat at the cafe, and the Guardians had also gone past him without stopping. As they neared Lacton, the Guardians were involved in a battle with the Rochgwars there and captured. Dulnas and Wistan were also captured when they presented themselves at the base. Then Gravelburn had arrived; he had thought that he would be in charge of the Rochgwars, but somebody by the shadowy name of Eritnorg was already entrenched as the leader there. The Rochgwars were confused about who their real leader was, because of the made-up prophecy.

Now back to the story!

Sing for Your Supper

The last time we left the Guardians, they were in the cage. Dulnas, Fil, Cut and Heath were still fighting. 'Happy birthday!' roared Heath. 'Have your presents! Here's a box!' Dulnas received a fist-sized imprint on his cheek from a punch. Cut got kicked and Fil got punched. The rest of Power Unit were still discussing the situation with Wistan.

'Any plans, guys?' asked Slick.

'How about we try to break the bars?' uttered a busy voice.

'The bars aren't made of cardboard, Heath.'

'Fine,' Heath replied, and then resumed his fight with the others.

'Or how about we pick the lock?'

'Does anyone have any hairpins?' asked Slick.

They all gave him a look that sarcastically suggested, 'Yeah, we take real good care of our hair, and we always carry our hairpins.'

Suddenly, Ember remembered something. 'Has anyone seen the owl?' he asked.

'The one that fell from the sky?' someone else asked. 'Isn't he still in Robin's bag, asleep?'

They looked over at Finn, who was indeed still asleep. Robin was cuddling the owl like a little soft toy. When the Guardians tried to lift up his arm, he would jerk it back to his original, comfortable position. Finn was asleep too, nicely snuggled up to Robin.

'Why don't we send the owl back to Delton?' Ember asked and was about to elaborate further, but Wistan clamped his mouth shut and interrupted him, 'Are you crazy? Last time he was heading for the fork, a short distance, and he went wrong. And now you want him to go even further to Delton? He'll probably end up somewhere different! Owls are not made for navigation!'

'Pigeons are the best navigators,' someone suggested.

'Dolphins!'

'Geese!'

The Guardians were still arguing when the Rochgwars arrived. 'Time for the singing lesson!' said a toothless Rochgwar. Another enthusiastic one said, 'We'll teach them some Rochgwarian kissy kissy love songs!' and the others around him squealed with embarrassed delight.

'Ew ...' groaned Cut. 'I don't want to sing those silly love songs.' He recoiled in horror.

'Ahem! Repeat after me!' announced a third Rochgwar.

Wi me don da banshee
Mi da cyclops

Some Guardians tried to copy the unfamiliar singing, and sang:

Me melon la can she
Me ga cyclops

'Tee hee!' laughed Heath out loud. 'These lyrics are really funny and silly!'

'Yeah!' giggled Cut.

'Silence, you ignorant brutes! You must learn to sing!' one of the Rochgwar instructors ordered.

Nitro looked insulted. His face bore the look of hurt.

'My mum always said I was a beautiful baby,' he protested. 'Not a brute.' He was definitely offended. 'How dare you. How very dare you!'

The Rochgwars tried again. 'Sing!' they commanded. But this time, none of the Guardians spoke up, and all around there was just confused silence.

'Gah! Let's give up on that song.' The Rochgwars realised there was no point in persisting. 'Now try this:

Grun tidium
Grun tidium
From Rochg Infini we come
Who made us?
Who made us?
Why, Great Rochg Infini!

'It's going to be a long day ...' said Slick under his breath as he tried half-heartedly.

The Guardians looked glum. 'This is so boring!' said Jack.

'My brain might melt from overload!' protested Ember.

This time the Rochgwars looked offended. 'What's wrong with our songs?' asked one.

Another glared at the Guardians and stated, 'Our songs were passed down from generation to generation. If you think you can do a better job, and your Guardian songs are better, then you sing, you toads!'

Some of the Guardians responded to the challenge.

'Okay!' Fil erupted into a rock (get it?) song in which he yelled at the top of his voice.

The Rochgwars stood entrenched and listened, admiring Fil, until Cut interjected and said, 'I can do much better that that!' and launched into a cheesy folk song.

'Alas, thy love is dear to me
And if thou didst intendeth ...'

'STOPPPPPPPPPP!' the Rochgwars begged.

'How about I –' Slick offered.

'Enough!' yelled a Rochgwar. 'You are all probably terrible. Except maybe this one,' he said, pointing at Fil. Fil looked a bit hopeful. But then the Rochgwar snapped out of his daydream and said, 'Actually, you were all bad! But you'll make good targets for target practice. *Arghahahahaha!* Good targets indeed!'

Then the Rochgwars slid opened the cage door and

threw in a big bag at the Guardians. 'Now eat!'

The hungry Guardians ripped open the bag and stuffed their mouths eagerly. Then Dulnas looked at the label at one corner of the bag and asked, 'What does "compost" mean?'

*   *   *

The next day the Rochgwars came back. 'Time for your daily singing lesson!' said one cheerfully.

'Okay,' said another, before offering a theory. 'We think the reason you lot were rubbish yesterday was because you did not do any warm-ups. So today – we'll start with warm-ups!

'First, we'll put our hands on our hips and breathe in and out! Like this!' The Rochgwar demonstrated and then turned to the Guardians, expecting them to follow. They exchanged glances and tried their best to copy. Robin looked uneasy.

Next the Rochgwar said, 'Now we'll roll our tongues to loosen them. We'll roll the 'R's – for Rochgwar. Like this. *Sssssss!'*

'But '*sssss'* is not the sound the letter R makes,' Cut pointed out.

'Oh, sorry, I don't know my letters,' the Rochgwar apologised.

'If *ssss* was the sound of the letter 'R', you'd all be Sochgwars!' laughed Heath. All the Guardians chuckled, together with a lone Rochgwar who had found the joke funny.

'Haha! That's a good one!' the Rochgwar laughed. But then he noticed the glare of his comrades and stopped abruptly.

'And Robin would really be "Sobin" – get it, "sobbing", boo boo hoo?' continued Heath.

Robin looked indignant. 'Give me some respect!'

'Do you really mean "serpect"?' Heath roared with

laughter and nearly fell over. This continual teasing of Robin was really funny for him.

The Rochgwars took one look at the Guardians, who were now roaring with laughter, substituting the letters in each other's names.

'Nitso!'

'Wirtan!'

'Dulnar!'

'They're no good for singing,' one of the Rochgwars decided, and they all stomped off.

Realisation

The next day, the Guardians were visited by Gravelburn and Eritnorg. As the pair made their way to the cage, Eritnorg, who was walking ahead, saw that the Guardians were squabbling amongst themselves. This annoyed him very much.

'Stop fighting, you lot!' he commanded sharply.

'As if we'll listen to you!' they retorted and returned to what they were doing.

'He does have a point. Stop right now!' a voice familiar cried out.

The Guardians recognised the familiar voice, and it surprised them. They immediately stopped what they were doing and turned to face the speaker. Gravelburn surveyed the scene in front of him. The eight Power Unit commanders, and the two scouts, Dulnas and Wistan, all locked up in a cage, like birds that could not fly away. All they could possibly do in the cage was ...

sing.

The Guardians could not believe their eyes. It really was Gravelburn.

The silence was broken by Wistan. 'Aha! I knew it! I was right! My message said Gravelburn was ahead of us, and he was!' he said smugly.

Eritnorg ignored him and turned to Gravelburn instead. 'So,' he drawled, 'these fleshlings listen not to me, but to you.' He took a deep breath and exhaled. 'You must be quite a bit of a something,' he concluded.

Gravelburn looked Eritnorg in the one eye. 'The Rochgwars here listen to you unquestioningly. I would say you are a bit of a something yourself too.'

All parties looked at one another in silence, each waiting for someone else to make the first move. Finally Eritnorg piped up, 'Do I have all members of that Power Unit here?'

'That's right,' confirmed Gravelburn.

'Yes! Yes! Mega yes!' Eritnorg celebrated. 'A few days ago I was in a rage, now I have Power Unit locked up in a cage!'

The Guardians looked at Eritnorg. 'You are such a poet,' said Heath, politely applauding.

The last time the Guardians had seen Gravelburn, the roles were reversed: Gravelburn was locked up in a cage being tortured by Nitro's I-Spy games. Now it was turn of the Guardians to be held prisoner, and tortured daily by the sound of Rochgwars singing.

'How long will we be kept in here for?' the Guardians demanded to know.

'After the talent show,' sneered Eritnorg. *Talent show?* Robin had a feeling that nothing good would come out of this.

'What talent show?' he asked.

'The one you have to do in a few days,' said Eritnorg, 'to earn your freedom. Give me and my Rochgwars a good show, and I'll let you go.'

With that, Eritnorg and Gravelburn turned and strode off.

They walked on in silence, each deep in his own thoughts.

'Hmm ... what is Eritnorg trying to achieve?' wondered Gravelburn. Was he really that interested in a talent show? Was he actually just trying to embarrass the Guardians before setting them free?

Gravelburn ran things over in his mind. Eritnorg had Power Unit trapped. Gravelburn knew Eritnorg way back from the time when he was Grontire, and he knew that he would never give freedom away so easily like that. The Guardians would never get their freedom back, at least not just for performing at a talent show.

Maybe, just maybe, Gravelburn pondered, *all Eritnorg wants is to continually keep the Guardians as hostages.* Maybe Eritnorg wanted more Guardians from Delton to launch rescue parties, and he would capture these

Guardians with the help of the Rochgwars nobody knew existed. Would he make these captives perform at future talent shows? Gravelburn recoiled at the idea. The Rochgwars would love that though. They would think the best of Eritnorg for continually providing them with entertainment.

More hostages ... more rescuers ... more rescuers being hostages ... more talent shows ... more adulation for Eritnorg ...the number of Guardians at Delton would dwindle, making it ripe for a takeover by ... Eritnorg. And the Rochgwars would pledge their loyalty to ... Eritnorg.

Gravelburn was confused. He had escaped from Delton and come to Lacton seeking to establish himself as leader of the Rochgwars there. But he had not expected to find them loyal to his old adversary, Grontire/Eritnorg, who had now captured his enemies, the Guardians. Eritnorg, to his followers, now seemed even more invincible, now that he had the Guardians, and was supposedly in charge of Gravelburn, the prophetic Chosen One. And they would stay loyal to him as long as the Guardians remained trapped in the camp, because it gave them something to cheer about, and to believe that Eritnorg was really great, and in charge.

Gravelburn realised that for him to take control of the Rochgwars, he had to start first by setting the Guardians free. It was a strange conclusion. The Guardians had tried to capture him. They had been obstacles in his plan for world domination. And now that they were captured and prisoners in a cold cage in Lacton, with no means of escape, they were still obstacles in his plan for world domination!

The dismantling of Eritnorg's power had already begun in Gravelburn's mind. It started out as a little flicker of hope, like a little match trying to be lit in a storm, and it grew to a forest fire. Gravelburn could feel the warmth of a hopeful future running through his veins.

'What are you smiling so happily about?' Eritnorg had noticed a strange glow to Gravelburn.

'The talent show,' Gravelburn lied.

The Talent Show

'Can we trust them?' thought Slick aloud. 'They want us to do some talent show, and if we give them a good one, they'll let us go?' He wasn't exactly sure, but he was quite confident that Rochgwars seldom kept their promises.

'If you're not certain, then don't take part in the talent show! They'll let the rest of us go, and they'll keep you here by yourself until you participate!' grumbled Dulnas.

'Well, what choice do we have?' asked Heath. 'Let's just amuse them, they'll have a good laugh, and then let us go!'

'Better idea – let's just escape when they take us out of this cage!' Fil suggested.

'There are hundreds of Rochgwars here, and only ten of us. If we do that, then we must be cau – ow!' Fil had just introduced his hand to Ember's mouth.

'Before we do that, let's send the owl to Delton with a message for help! That would be wise,' Cut pointed out.

'There's no way you're sending my partner back to Delton!' Robin protested angrily.

'What do you mean, your partner?' questioned Slick.

'He's going to be my partner when I do owlery – for the talent show!'

'Don't tell me you're on board for the talent show now, Robin,' groaned Nitro.

'I spy ... a spoilsport!' retorted Robin.

The discussion soon turned to what everyone would do for their act in the talent show.

'Do you think I should do jokes for the show?' asked Heath.

'Maybe,' someone answered, concerned about their own act.

'Then I'll need an assistant to play dumb. What about you, Nitro?' continued Heath. Nitro had slinked into a corner.

'We'll do a fight demonstration with sticks!' said Fil and Cut eagerly.

'And I'll do a talk on catapult safety,' Ember decided.

'And you'll all also practise singing Rochgwar songs until the singing is perfect!' growling voices declared. The Guardians turned around to face a band of approaching Rochgwars. It was time for another daily singing lesson.

*   *   *

Soon it was the day of the talent show. 'I'm really excited about this!' said a Rochgwar. 'I've been waiting for a show like this for a long time!'

'I hope they've memorised the words to the songs!' said another Rochgwar hopefully. 'We've spent so much time and effort trying to teach them! The least they could do would be to give a good rendition of our songs!'

'I've been keeping chickens,' said a third. 'I've got plenty of eggs. My friends will get ten eggs each!' Suddenly, everyone flocked to be this Rochgwar's best mate.

Most of the Guardians were also feeling the tension and excitement of the moment. But not everyone was happy about the talent show. Nitro's and Jack's faces told a different story.

'I'm not performing. I said, I'm not performing.'

'I also don't want to do it.'

'I'm getting a touch of stage fright!' worried Ember, hoping that he had remembered his points properly.

'Now remember, guys, after this talent show, they've promised to let us go,' Robin reminded them all. 'If they don't let us go at the end, then get ready to run for it!'

'Why don't we just run for it now? For the last time ...
they! Are! Not! Going! To! Let! Us! Go!' said Nitro,
spitting out every word.

'Yeah!' piped up Jack in agreement.

The Guardians were led out to a makeshift platform in
the middle of Lacton. It was just a heap of old planks
laid in a haphazard criss-cross pattern, but it was large
enough that they could all stand on it. As they came
under the watchful eyes of the excited Rochgwars, they
saw Eritnorg seated in one corner in a decorative chair,
next to Gravelburn, although it was hard for him to look
impressive when seated on a wooden chair decorated
with stickers of hearts and stars.

The assembled Rochgwars were rubbing their hands
with glee. Most of them were sat down, watching the
Guardians getting ready. Other Rochgwars were
already picking up eggs from nearby baskets and
practising their aim on a painted wooden target.

Gravelburn wasn't all that bothered about the talent show, especially one featuring his old enemies, but for all the trouble they had caused him in the past, he wasn't going to pass up the chance to throw eggs at them. He and Eritnorg had their individual baskets between their chairs.

*   *   *

First up was Robin. He came to the centre of the platform and exclaimed, 'I'm very excited to show you my new trick. Enjoy!' He had a wide smile across his face and his heart was beating fast.

'*Ged on wid it!*' Some Rochgwars already had their eggs poised and ready to go, and their faces looked very impatient.

'Okay, okay, okay,' said Robin, slightly flustered. He held out one arm outstretched.

'*Is dat it?*' scoffed the Rochgwars. One Rochgwar threw his egg at Robin but it missed. Robin, though, hadn't noticed. After a few seconds, Robin put a few pieces of

141

bread on his arm. Suddenly, Finn descended from out of nowhere, landed on Robin's arm, gobbled up the bread, before moving from one leg to the other and waving his claws around. Robin felt very, very proud of his own owlery skills.

'Surely they'll let me go now after they've seen this trick?' he thought as he bowed. As he returned to his upright position, an egg splattered on his face. *What was that all about?*

'Why is he bowing?' wondered Finn. 'He hasn't been doing anything, he's just been standing there while I've been doing the hard work. And why are they clapping him? I thought this was supposed to be a talon show, and he has none.'

Finn continued waving his claws around on Robin's outstretched arm while Robin was pelted with eggs and his face was streaked with yellow. Robin found himself filling up with rage.

'Why did you all do that?' he shouted.

'Um ... this is what we do when we get egg-cited!' offered a Rochgwar as an explanation.

Finn got bored of showing off his talons and flew away. The other Guardians looked at Robin and were rolling around, hysterical with laughter, at the sight of him covered in yellow. It wasn't every day that Captain Robin got pelted with eggs.

'I spy, with my little eye, something beginning with 'e'!' shouted Nitro, stating the obvious.

Next up was Ember. But after he saw what had happened to Robin, he felt a little nervous ... but at the same time confident that the Rochgwars would find the information he had to really offer useful and learn something from it. The faces of the Rochgwars suggested that they thought that the next act was going to be a waste of time.

'*Dis one had been better be gud!*' said a Rochgwar.

'*Better no fly fly bird again – or else!*' warned another.

'*Hu haf moor egg?*' asked a third.

'*Mi not many left. But take dees ones here,*' answered a fourth, passing over some.

Ember began by addressing the Rochgwars. 'There are many dangerous and sharp objects here in this camp which may cause injury ...'

The Rochgwars were puzzled. 'Huh?' said one. '*Dis joke?"* grunted a second.

Ember continued. 'Some of the more dangerous objects in this camp include swords and catapults. I can tell you the way to ensure accidents do not happen. Here are some health and safety tips.

'For swords, the sharp point of the blade can cause serious injury. So make sure you continually keep a sword sheathed when it is not in use. You may also prefer not to sharpen your sword too sharply, keeping it blunt so you do not accidentally injure someone.

'Now we move on to the next point. A bigger dangerous

weapon is the catapult. Now, there are many catapults in this camp so please take note. You could easily fall into it and fire it by accident. This would mean that you might launch yourself far over the walls. You might want to consider disabling the firing mechanism for catapults not in use. Or perhaps adjust the position of the lever so that the range is limited and causes less injury.'

Ember paused for a moment and studied his audience. 'Right, are you taking this all in? Take notes if you need to, I have a lot to get through and that was only parts one and two of a hundred. Shall we move on to the next part?'

The Rochgwars had had enough. They had waited as patiently as they could. 'Egg time!' one suddenly shouted and the others followed like a dam had burst from waves of pent-up frustration. Ember was splattered by eggs.

*   *   *

Heath was nominated to go next after Ember. He was a bundle of energy and tried to lift the energy of the crowd after it had been drained. 'Hey guys! How's it going? All good? Y'all looking rock solid today!'

He paused and tried to judge the mood of the Rochgwars. No response.

'Anyway, today I'm going to tell you my best jokes! Whadyya say to that?' The energy from Heath was similar to the energy in a rock concert. But the energy he was getting back from the Rochgwars was like lead.

'Right!' said Heath. 'Joke time! Why did 4 cross the road? 2 get 2 the other side!'

'Urrrr?!' replied some of the Rochgwars, scratching their heads. Heath sighed.

'2 and 2 make 4. Get it?'

'No!' growled a Rochgwar. 'Two and two make tutu! Not four!' He rose, annoyed, and some around him had to restrain him and sit him down.

'Okay, okay, maybe let's leave that one and move on.

146

Let's try another,' Heath continued. 'Knock knock!'

'Yay!' cried a Rochgwar. 'More Guardians!'

'Knock knock!' Heath tried again.

'You have more Guardians?'

'Arrrgh!' exploded Heath. 'Never mind – how do you spell candy in two letters?'

'Huh???' murmured a few voices in low growls.

''C' and 'Y',' answered Heath. 'Because, you know, 'candy' is spel ... never mind.'

He moved on quickly from joke to joke. 'When is a door not a door? When it's ajar!'

'*Me no geddit!*' wailed a frustrated Rochgwar who was on the verge of tears.

'Okay, okay – try this one. How does a grizzly catch a

fish? With his bear hands!'

If Heath had been expecting the Rochgwars to get his jokes, he was severely disappointed. But suddenly one Rochgwar jumped to his feet. 'Ooo! Ooo!' the Rochgwar cried, all excited, as if he had grasped the logic.

'Yes ... ?' said Heath, hoping the Rochgwar would explain the riddle to the others.

'Why did the Rochgwar throw his egg?' asked the Rochgwar instead.

'I don't know – why did the Rochgwar throw his egg?' Heath replied.

'Because the act was rubbish!'

Heath pondered for a moment. 'But the punchline doesn't make sense!' he protested as the first shower of eggs fell.

Waiting in the wings, some of the remaining Guardians looked nervous. 'You next! Get ready!' said a

Rochgwar, gesturing at Jack, who was chewing his nails.

'I don't want to do it!' cried Jack. 'I don't want to do it!'

'Gwahahaha!' laughed Nitro at the sight of Heath. He just couldn't help it.

*   *   *

Fil, Cut, Wistan and Dulnas ended up going instead of Jack. '*Yoo show gud! Yoo badder maike gud show!*' growled the Rochgwar in charge of the prisoners/contestants as he hustled them out of the cage.

'Yeah, yeah, okay, okay,' said Fil, like someone who has been given the same instructions many times over. He turned to the others. 'Who's got the sticks?'

'You were supposed to bring them!' cried Wistan.

'Oh ...' Fil answered. He turned to the guard. 'Mister Rochgwar?'

'Uhh?!'

'Permission to get some props?'

'Go.' The Rochgwar grunted and granted permission.

Fil made his way to the crowd and picked up a few sticks belonging to members of the audience. Some of them were a bit puzzled. They thought they were going to watch a magic show.

'Hey guys!' shouted Fil to the crowd after he had made his way back to the others. 'How's it going? Right, right, today we're going to show you a fight demonstration; basic attack and defence tactics of the Delton Guardians.

'Is it wise to reveal our fighting tactics to our enemies?' Ember wondered off-stage, in a cloak of crusted yellow.

'Guys, grab these!' he said as he tossed them at the others. Dulnas, Wistan and Cut grabbed them in mid-air. Cut felt really excited as he held on to his weapon.

Fil turned to the Rochgwars and explained, 'Whoever gets tapped three times is out!'

'Tee hee!' whispered Cut. 'I'm going to defeat everyone!' He so wanted to win.

'Ready? Start!' shouted Fil and he proceeded to give a running commentary of the events as the others began stick-fighting.

'Ooh, look, Dulnas is defending against Cut with a single Honey Cake Curtain Draw! And Cut is furiously bashing with a Birthday Bammer!'

'Yaah!' yelled Cut as he bashed his stick against Dulnas.

This got the attention of the Rochgwars. This was no silly magic show. It was a good old-fashioned fight, just how they liked it. They all cheered and whooped. This was the best act of the talent show!

'Fight! Fight! Fight! Fight!' Chants rang out among the audience.

The demonstrating Guardians really got into it.

Suddenly, Dulnas gulped as a crack appeared in his stick.

'Oh, what's happened there?' commented Fil, drawing the audience's attention to Dulnas. The Rochgwars gasped collectively. 'But wait – wow! Dulnas is actually holding out even though his stick is breaking! He actually got Cut once! Dulnas has switched from being on the defensive, and is now on the offensive! Cut has sustained a hit and is now on two lives! This is exciting! If this continues, Cut is in danger of being out! Great move, Dulnas! Come on, Dulnas! What could go wro –'

Dulnas's stick broke and split in two just as Cut parried away an attack. Dulnas froze in his stance. His face sank.

'Oh dear!' Fil continued, whipping up the excitement of the crowd. 'His stick broke! His stick broke!' Fil roared, as if the Rochgwars hadn't noticed that already. They whooped with delight and excitement. 'What an unexpected turn of events!'

Now Dulnas was getting chased by Cut all around the makeshift arena. Fil continued stating the obvious. 'Oh, now Dulnas is getting chased by Cut around –'

'Ahhhhhhhhh!' screamed Dulnas, with Cut in pursuit.

The Rochgwars roared their approval.

'Grahahahaha!'

'Dees rilee fhuny!'

'Geddim, two-hit boy! Geddim!'

In the end, Dulnas ran out of breath from the pursuit and had to pause for rest. Immediately, Cut pounced and tapped him three times to signify three hits. 'One! Two! Three!'

'Awww ...' wailed Dulnas in between gasps for breath.

'But I wanted to win in this demonstration!'

Cut flexed his muscles to the Rochgwars. He yelled to the cheering crowd, 'I am – the champioooooon ...'

Suddenly, a cry of 'strike' rang out. It was Wistan who had scored a hit on Cut. Everyone had been so transfixed by the Dulnas-Cut fight, they had forgotten about Wistan who had been hiding in one corner all the time. Even Fil, the commentator.

'Oh no, Cut's got another hit. That's two hits on him now – one from Dulnas and one from Wistan. He's got one life left. But he's furiously slashing with a Triple Gummy Bear 180 Twist!'

'Woooo!' cried the Rochgwars appreciatively. They were certainly being entertained and educated by the Guardian fighting moves on display here.

'Oh! Oh! Whoa! That's a strike for Wistan there! Cut has lost all his lives! It's a win for Wistan! Give it up for your champiooooon ...'

The Rochgwars stood up and roared. It was hard to tell if they were applauding Wistan or applauding the whole act, but they were definitely very excited by the fight demonstration. And you should know by now, reader, that there's one thing Rochgwars do when they're excited. They started launching eggs at the four Guardians who had just completed their act. Even Fil, who had not been in the actual fight but on the side commentating, was not spared.

Egg after egg was launched. Some Rochgwars threw their eggs wildly. Others took careful aim, lining up the egg with a Guardian nose, before launching them. Smarter Rochgwars aimed for the top of a Guardian head, to allow for the effect of gravity, so that the egg would dip in its flight and eventually end up on a face.

It wasn't just the four Guardians in the last act that the Rochgwars were aiming for. Soon all the ten Guardians saw missiles flying at them which crunched on impact and released yellow dribble. Finn the owl took off in flight. Or maybe fright.

155

'Oi!' yelled Slick in angry protest. After all, no one likes to be a target board. 'Why are you doing that?' he yelled at the Rochgwars.

'Wasn't it a good act?' Robin spoke up, defending his four friends, and also protecting himself from the flying eggs which the Rochgwars never seemed to run out off.

Jack's hair was covered in egg shampoo and crust. 'I wasn't even involved in that act! It's not fair! I don't even want to do this talent show!'

'Ooh, yes, right, but this is how we show we are excited and approve!' answered some of the Rochgwars.

In the end, all the Guardians were covered in yolk and shell fragments.

'Yeahhhhh!' roared the Rochgwars. 'Great target practice! Thank you, Eritnorg!' They turned to face their leader as he rose from his wooden seat to acknowledge the cheers and applause, and continued as he made his way down to give a speech.

A chant spread across Lacton. 'Eritnorg! Eritnorg! Eritnorg!'

'Hang on, it was actually I that suggested the talent show,' pointed out Gratin, but he could not be heard over the Rochgwars, although Gravelburn noticed.

Eritnorg stood in front of the pelted Guardians and waved his hands for silence.

'Fellow Rochgwars! Our camp had been stripped of joy. It was a cold, dark place. But that's how it should be! Cold! Cruel! *Arghahahaha!* We are Rochgwars, after all! But then these 'visitors' arrived, and while I hate to say this, they have brought some joy to our camp. Tonight, there has been joyful shouting. Tonight, there has been great excitement. Tonight, there has been laughter amongst us. Tonight, there has been plenty of egg throwing. Tonight, there has been –'

'Can we go now?' interrupted Slick. He was tired of listening to speeches. But his protests fell on deaf ears. Eritnorg carried on. 'Tonight, we've had so much fun.' He waited for the cheering of the Rochgwars to die down into complete silence. Then he paused for effect and to command the attention of every single Rochgwar under his leadership.

'So … who would like next to hear a song!'

'Yeeeeeah!' the Rochgwars erupted. They had thought that the entertainment was coming to an end, but there was actually more! So that was why Eritnorg was making the Guardians learn songs for! He'd actually had this all planned out! He wanted the Guardians to entertain the Rochgwars. What a great leader, always thinking of his troops and making sure they were well looked after!

'Eritnorg's the best! Eritnorg's the best!' Both the Guardians and Gravelburn looked visibly irritated as Eritnorg milked the attention and applause.

The irritation and frustration of some of the Guardians turned to horror. They were all covered in egg yolk and shells, and had performed for the Rochgwars, but this was not the end of it?

The Rochgwars were now chanting as loudly as they could, *'Wewansong! Wewansong! Wewansong!'* The chanting grew frenzied and disjointed so it sounded at times like *'Wewanwee! Wansongwe! Songwewe!'* The Rochgwars also readied more eggs in their hands in case the Guardians were going to disagree.

The Guardians felt they had no choice. 'Do you remember anything they have been teaching us?' asked Fil to no one in particular.

'Not really,' answered Slick.

'Dear heavens, stop worrying; just scream random noises, loudly, and with style!' shouted Robin, frustrated by the turn of events. 'These monsters don't really understand anything, and besides, they wouldn't be able to hear us clearly anyway!'

The audience was getting impatient. *'Wewansongnow! Wewansongnow!'* The intolerant cries of the rock monsters grew intimidatingly, like a chorus of grumbles that threatened to erupt at any moment.

The Guardians lined up in a row and opened their mouths. '*Ent sobut tion he bot ...*'

Their voices were flat and sounded terrible. Eggs flew across the arena. *Thwack! Thwack!* Even Eritnorg had to scramble away from the platform to avoid being hit.

'Either we're really bad, or we're really good!' announced Nitro cheerfully.

The Guardians kept singing as best as they could. The din grew louder and louder.

'*Sink ichunk book downs ...*'

The Rochgwars threw more eggs but had soon run out. It didn't stop them from shouting though. What was it that these silly human children were mouthing? How dare they disgrace the beautiful Rochgwarian lyrics? Did they not remember anything from all that time they were being taught? What a waste of time!

Rescue Party

Dear reader, you might also be wondering at this point, 'Didn't anyone at Delton notice that Power Unit had been gone for a long time? Did anyone notice Power Unit was missing?'

(What's that? No? You didn't wonder about it? You were just happy reading about the talent show? Oh that's fine, it doesn't matter then. Just pretend you did.)

Anyway, the disappearance of Power Unit was noticed back in Delton, so they sent a team of their best scouts to look for them. These scouts were led by Lex Cerberus and Hinx Matr. The former was a highly-trained scout, skilled in the Delton Guardian art of, um, tree-climbing. (Actually it's not an art, Lex claims it is, just to show off.) Lex had distinguished himself in the defence of Delton when Gravelburn had previously attacked, accurately aiming arrow after arrow at Rochgwars.

Hinx Matr, similarly, was a good archer. He was not

only good with longbows, but also with crossbows, and had once killed an earthworm from two hundred paces away in an archery lesson he was teaching. He had explained afterwards to the watching students that arrows are pulled downwards by gravity over the course of their flight, and that there was also a breeze from the west, so while it had looked like he had missed the big circular target board they were all looking at, he was only pretending to aim at it to compensate for the gravity and wind, to get his real target, the earthworm.

The scouts had tracked Power Unit all the way to Lacton. They were aided along the way by a tavern owner who claimed that all his food had been eaten by a small rocky being.

The two leaders left their team at the base of Lacton Hill. They told them to take cover there and prepare for defensive action, while they, the leaders, would scout ahead.

The two of them lay prone on the ground and slowly crawled up the hill, keeping a low profile so that they would not be noticed. They moved slowly and

162

deliberately, so that there would be no sounds to alert anyone and give them away. Every now and then, however, the sharp tip of Hinx's longbow would poke Lex in the eye. If anyone had been nearby, they would have heard intermittent cries of 'Ow! Ow! Ow!' in the dark and largely silent night.

Eventually the duo got to the top of the hill. They could hear loud shouting coming from within Lacton, so they needn't have worried about being spotted on the way up. They also need not have worried about how to make their way in, because the door was hanging off his hinges after Gravelburn had barged his way in. A small pile of rocks lay by the door. They crept past the door and tried to observe events within Lacton.

'Sounds like a celebration,' Lex whispered, indicating ahead. They could both see a large group of Rochgwars with their backs turned to them. The Rochgwars were watching something, and excited about it.

'Let's hope it's not a human sacrifice,' Hinx answered darkly.

163

They paused briefly to observe before Lex stated the obvious.

'What are Rochgwars doing here? Where are the Lacton Guardians?'

'Never mind the Rochgwars, what about Power Unit?'

'Do you see them?'

'Naw ... not yet anyway. But they must be here. I think that's what these monsters are cheering about. We need to get to a better position.'

They spotted a catapult in its resting position and stealthily darted across the ground towards it. Lex slowly climbed up to the highest point, hoping he would be able to see above the rows of Rochgwars from the rock basket.

He did. And he was shocked by what he saw. He counted ten junior Guardians, all barely recognisable with messy heads of yellow, standing in a line, being cheered by Rochgwars. The Guardians were roaring at the top of their voices.

They were singing Rochgwar songs.

'What can you see?' asked Hinx from below.

'They've been brainwashed,' answered Lex, horrified.
They retreated to fetch their troops.

Happiness

Robin was not happy. Not at all. He felt he had already done his part in the talent show. He wasn't naturally good with owls, and owls didn't naturally like him, but he had tried to perform something of interest with Finn – but had got egged.

He had quietly watched the fight demonstration between four of his fellow Guardians, hadn't interfered by asking questions like 'Do you think we should be showing our special manoeuvres to our enemies?' – but he had got egged.

He thought that the Guardians would go free after they had entertained the Rochgwars, but no, they were made to sing a song in a language unfamiliar to him. He would have preferred to sing his all-time favourite song, *Delton in the Night*. It goes like this:

Oh what a sight
Like the Northern Lights
It's Delton in the Night!

It's a sight I admire
As I sit by the fire
It's Delton in the night!

After we had been walking
We all sat down talking
In Delton in the night!

I said before we parted,
I think somebody ...
In Delton in the night!

I hope you all keep well,
Even though there's a strange smell,
In Delton in the night!

He thought the Rochgwars songs they had been made to learn were all silly. So even though singing and languages were not his best points, he had tried – but had got egged.

Robin made up his mind. After this was all over, he would definitely have to write a new song, with this as an opening:

This show was fake
We all got egged
In Lacton in the night!

That thought kept him happy.

*   *   *

Gratin was also not happy. Yes, he had been promoted to the rank of lieutenant, but what good was that? It wasn't a very high rank, in his opinion. He also felt a sense of injustice that his idea had been stolen. He would have traded rank for the fame and the admiration of his fellow Rochgwars, instead of being a lousy lieutenant that nobody was going to listen to anyway. Who was going to listen to lowly Lieutenant Gratin, when all the Rochgwars cared about was Eritnorg?

Gratin fumed as he watched Eritnorg receive the adulation of the troops. The idea for the talent show had been his, but Eritnorg was now pretending he had come up with it and was being treated like a god by the Rochgwars. They were all shouting his name! Gratin

168

could have been shouting, 'It was my idea actually!' at the top of his voice but nobody would have heard him. He was very, very jealous as he watched Eritnorg. The cheers of the Rochgwars should have been for him!

*   *   *

Gravelburn was also not pleased. Eritnorg was the favourite of the troops now. Gravelburn had come to Lacton to gather troops to take revenge of the Guardians, but it didn't look like he was going to get them to follow and obey him, because they were too enthralled with Eritnorg. *Hmmmph!* Eritnorg could sneeze, and they would cheer, Gravelburn thought. He could sing badly, and they would cheer. He would shout and make a lot of noise, and they would cheer. He could tell bad jokes, and they would cheer. He could click his fingers, and they would cheer. Eritnorg could do anything, and no matter how badly he did it, he would still have the Rochgwars eating out of his hand.

Gravelburn made his way down to Gratin.

'So,' said Gratin, looking at Gravelburn. 'Seven full

moons ago you were a prisoner in a cell. Now you are the Chosen One, and second in command to Eritnorg. Not bad.'

'So, how have you been since I saw you last?' asked Gravelburn.

'The last time we saw each other,' reminded Gratin bluntly, 'we were staring at each other's fists, and you punched me to pieces. So much for friendship.'

'I had no choice,' Gravelburn protested. 'It was you or me. He,' Gravelburn said, gesturing at Eritnorg, 'was the one that made us punch each other repeatedly until one of us was smashed into pieces. I didn't want to do it, but I had to. I did make sure that there many large-sized pieces of you left for you to respawn though.'

'Thank you for ensuring that,' Gratin replied. 'I owe you something for the chance to respawn, instead of being destroyed completely forever.'

'I wasn't destroying you,' Gravelburn explained to Gratin. 'I was saving you by making sure you weren't around, and that you wouldn't have to take part in the final assault on Lacton, when the chances of being destroyed were very high. I broke you up, so you could avoid it and respawn after all that was over. Most of our friends who took part in that battle are no longer with us today; they were all smashed to tiny fragments in the explosions and perished.'

They watched Eritnorg continue to address the Rochgwars, in front of the Guardians, a sea of yellow goo and shell fragments.

'We need to do something about this,' said Gravelburn.

'Indeed,' Gratin replied.

*   *   *

The only one who was pleased was Eritnorg. He had called a meeting because he wanted to get a few ideas. While all the other Rochgwar commanders' ideas were lousy, Gratin's had been perfect – so perfect that he had stolen it. And now Eritnorg was feeling smug. The Rochgwars were all chanting his name unanimously.

171

When he had first seen Gravelburn, he had panicked slightly, but now Gravelburn's presence at Lacton made things even better for him.

While the Rochgwars believed that Gravelburn was special because he was the Chosen One, Eritnorg was now greater than him, in their eyes, because Gravelburn had once been under his charge!

The arrival of the Guardians might also have been worrying, but now that it looked like Eritnorg had used them in the talent show to entertain the Rochgwars, everyone loved him even more!

Eritnorg addressed the assembled Rochgwars again. 'Great show, wasn't it? My Rochgwars ... *myyyyy* Rochgwars, I have treated you to a great show tonight. I have given you Guardians to sing and perform, and you have had fun with the eggs. The saying goes, 'All good things must come to an end' and I'm afraid this is true.' The faces of the Guardians lit up and they thought, 'Finally!'

Eritnorg continued, 'Tonight's entertainment is finished. No more. No more. *But would you like to have the same talent show again tomorrow*?' The Rochgwars, who had been listening quietly, erupted in a frenzy.

'Yerrrr!' they cheered and hooted. 'Excellent!'

The cries of 'Eritnorg! Eritnorg!' echoed once again around Lacton.

'Now take them back to the Kaje!' Eritnorg ordered. The Guardians were pushed and shoved all the way back to the cage by some burly Rochgwars.

'From north, south, east and west; I am definitely the best!'

Eritnorg was now even performing ad-libs to the crowd. This went on for quite a while, much to Gravelburn's annoyance.

The Guardians were back to where they had started ever since they had arrived in Lacton.

'Anyone got any ideas now?' asked Nitro, when they were all back in the cell. The sound of cheering Rochgwars could still be heard.

'I think tomorrow I might try doing owlery with two owls, if I can find another owl!' said Robin.

'I will give a talk on the dangers of plasters,' decided Ember.

'I still don't wanna do it!' protested Jack.

'No!' shouted Nitro angrily. 'Not ideas about the next talent show; ideas about how to get out of here!'

'Ohh .... no,' said Robin, rather sadly. Being cheered, even if by enemy Rochgwars, was starting to feel addictive. At least it seemed they appreciated him a bit more than the other members of Power Unit.

Nettles and White Spirit

Hinx Matr and Lex Cerberus had summoned their troops up to the entrance of Lacton. 'Hinx and I think Power Unit are in there,' Lex announced.

'Lex and I think that Power are in there,' Hinx confirmed. 'We think they are brainwashed.'

'We think they are brainwashed,' Lex explained.

'Stop copying what I say!' they both cried at the same time.

'Uh, sirs,' said a soldier, 'how can you both be sure that they are in Lacton?'

Lex and Hinx both explained the recent events.

'Here's the plan,' Lex said. 'I think there's a massive cage at the far end of this base. That's where they must be held. We'll go in and grab them out of it, while the Rochgwars are distracted, or asleep.'

'But sir, how do we convince them to come with us if they have been brainwashed?' piped up another soldier.

'I could be wrong,' Hinx said, 'but once I vaguely remember seeing a Delton Guardian student workbook with notes that said this: *anyone who has been brainwashed should have his or her head rubbed with nettles; the sting of the nettle will revive him or her from the brainwashed state.*'

'Are you sure?' Lex Cerberus asked.

'Got any better ideas?' Hinx Matr replied.

*   *   *

Gravelburn interrupted Eritnorg's moment of glory. 'Wait! It was a good show, but it's not over yet. The Chosen One hasn't yet performed. The Chosen One's act is not complete!'

The applause of the Rochgwars paused. Then it rose in volume again for Gravelburn when the Rochgwars

176

realised he was offering them more entertainment. There was more of the talent show and it had not yet finished!

'Gravelburn! Gravelburn! Chosen One! Chosen One!' the Rochgwars chorused.

Gravelburn stepped in front of Eritnorg and received the applause. 'I could get used to this,' he thought. 'This adulation is … befitting of me. Hmmm ...'

Behind him, Eritnorg fumed. 'Hmmm!!!!'

Gravelburn ordered John to move to a spot about ten paces ahead of him. John obeyed and hovered on the indicated spot, unsure of what was going to happen next. Then Gravelburn picked up a small rock and threw it directly at John. It passed through him and *thumped!* a Rochgwar on the other side.

'Ouch!' the Rochgwar cried.

'Whoa!' the assembled crowd of Rochgwars gasped. They could not believe what they had just seen.

John changed position and hovered in front of another Rochgwar. Gravelburn bent down to the ground and randomly picked up another fist-sized rock. He reared back, and launched the rock at John again. The rock passed right through him. Gravelburn had hurled it with such ferocity, the Rochgwar that it hit on the other side of John completely crumbled into pieces.

The watching Rochgwars were stunned. *How are the objects able to pass through the white spirit*, they wondered? They picked up rocks and other objects they could find and hurled them at John. The objects passed through him harmlessly, of course, but some of the Rochwars on the other side were hit. Rocks were then picked up by others to hurl. Every Rochgwar wanted to have a go at throwing things through the white spirit.

'Behold, Rochgwars, *myyyyyy* Rochgwar friends, *myyyyyyy* fellow Rochgwars,' Gravelburn announced. 'I am Gravelburn, the Chosen One, and I control the magic white spirit! Who wants to see the more of the magic white spirit – today, tomorrow, the next full moon?'

The Rochgwars roared with delight. Soon the echoing cries of 'Gravelburn! Gravelburn! Chosen One! Chosen One!' restarted as John zipped in front of various Rochgwars, daring them to hurl whatever objects they could find at him.

Spears, swords, maces, clubs and all sorts of weaponry flew through the air, either destroying those they hit, or angering those landed on into seeking revenge. Even Gravelburn was taking part. He found an unspoilt egg that must have either not broken on impact, or had not been used on the Guardians, and picked it up in his right hand.

John darted here and there, shouting 'Grush niem! Grush niem!' excitedly, sometimes teasing the Rochgwars by flying in front of them and watching them panic when they realised things were going to be hurled at them. He weaved here and there, and eventually found himself three paces in front of Eritnorg.

Eritnorg rolled his eyes. *Stupid floaty white thing.*

Gravelburn took a deep breath, and then hurled his egg

right at John.

With Friends Like These, Who Needs Enemies?

The egg passed through John and hit Eritnorg in the face. *Thwack!* It lodged itself in his eye socket. Eritrnorg was shocked at Gravelburn's actions and his anger bubbled up inside him. At first Eritnorg's face looked fine but slowly it looked like he was crying yellow tears which streaked down one side of his face. Eritnorg launched himself at John but just fell right through him and *splat!* onto the ground in front of Gravelburn. Gravelburn seized the chance and put his foot on Eritnorg's head disrespectfully.

'Gravelburn is always ... one step ahead!' he cried out.

Some Rochgwars gasped. 'The Chosen One has overthrown Eritnorg!' they said in disbelief.

Other Rochgwars were also shocked. 'How dare he do that to our dear Eritnorg!' they cried.

Eritnorg shook himself free, got to his feet and punched Gravelburn. Gravelburn reeled back and then gave Eritnorg the same treatment. The two traded blows, each realising that the winner would eventually take control of the Lacton Rochgwars.

Some Rochgwars tried to hold them back. 'Don't fight! If you both crumble, we'll have no leader!'

Other Rochgwars also fought amongst themselves. Some thought Gravelburn should now be the leader, because he had triumphed over Eritnorg, while others thought Eritnorg was still their leader. It was every Rochgwar for himself. In the fighting, many Rochgwars broke up into pieces which were then used and flung at others. Both sets of supporters did this. John continued floating in front of Rochgwars and around them.

While this was happening, nobody noticed Monty and Gratin slip off towards the Kaje with something shiny in Gratin's hands.

*   *   *

Hinx Matr, Lex Cerberus and their troops noticed a massive fight taking place. They also noted one tall Rochgwar and another short one slip away towards where they thought the cage was.

'Great,' thought Hinx. 'We'll have to fight them to free Power Unit.'

Inside the cage, the Guardians noticed two Rochgwars approaching. As they neared, the taller one reached for a set of keys and unlocked the gate – the other was too short. 'Follow me,' Gratin whispered. The Guardians didn't ask or argue and slipped out behind him and Monty.

The group slipped through fighting Rochgwars towards the entrance of Lacton.

'Aw ...' groaned Cut and Fil, surveying the scene around them. 'Could we not stay for a tiny bit longer? You know, to fight a few Rochgwars?'

'Don't be nuts!' scolded Robin.

'Be careful! We don't want them to know we have escaped,' piped up Ember.

Hinx Matr and Lex Cerberus saw Power Unit obediently following the tall and short Rochgwars. They turned to their troops. 'There they are! Our brainwashed junior Guardians are obediently following the Rochgwars. Ready your nettles! We're going to snatch them, rub the nettles on their heads, and then get out of here when they have been cleansed. The two of us will take care of the Rochgwars, you guys handle the nettling!'

They all charged forward in single file. Seeing the Guardians approaching, Gratin assumed they were rescuers so he and Monty walked off, leaving the captured Guardians alone to their rescuers. 'Whoa!' thought Hinx proudly in disbelief. 'Our reputation as fierce warriors is so great, the Rochgwars retreat when they see us!'

'Everyone!' Lex ordered his team. 'Grab a member of Power Unit. Or one of the other two. Remember to keep rubbing the nettles for one hundred times on the head. Don't stop even when they start to protest. In fact, the

184

more they protest, the harder you have to rub the nettles on their heads, to make sure it really works to overcome the brainwashing!'

It was Nitro who noticed Hinx Matr and Lex Cerberus rushing towards them. Finally! Rescue had come! After all that time in the cell, cold and hungry, and being forced to sing silly Rochgwar songs. The captured Guardians were ecstatic to be finally rescued and leave Lacton. They ran towards their rescuers. But before they knew it, they were each grabbed and forced to stop in their tracks. They each felt stinging on the top of the heads.

'Hey! What are you doing?' protested Slick.

The rescuers had each grabbed a junior Guardian in a headlock and was applying the cure for brainwashing.

'Ouch!' cried Fil.

'Why are you doing this! The pain, the pain!' shouted Cut, as he felt something painful against his scalp.

185

'Oi! What are you doing?' screamed Wistan and he kicked and punched.

The more the captured Guardians protested, the harder their rescuers rubbed the nettles on their heads. They tried to break free, but they more they tried, the more tightly their rescuers held on to them. Soon, scuffles broke out between both sets of Guardians. The ones who were trying to apply the cure for brainwashing were not happy with being hit or thrashed at. The one who were being 'rescued' were also not happy.

'Have you come to rescue us, or have you come to torture us?' said Robin.

'Ignore him,' ordered Hinx Matr. 'Keep nettling! It's for their own good!'

*   *   *

The commotion caused by the captured Guardians and their rescuers had not gone unnoticed. 'Guardians at the gate!' one Rochgwar alerted the others. Soon a swarm of them descended upon the Guardians.

'Keep nettling! We'll try to hold them off!' Lex Ceberus ordered.

'We're going to absolutely destroy you now!' one Rochgwar cruelly announced. Some of them bared their stony teeth and prepared to smash the Guardians into smithereens.

'Wait!' another Rochgwar cried out. 'These are the targets for Eritnorg's next talent show. They and the new ones must be protected and saved for the egging!' The Rochgwars that agreed with this then formed a line between the Guardians and the Rochgwars that wanted to attack them.

'Are you crazy?' the first Rochgwar that had spoken asked the second. 'The Guardians are our enemies!'

'Are you crazy?' the second Rochgwar replied. 'What is a talent show with no talent to throw eggs at?'

Amidst the Rochgwar disagreement, the rescuing Guardians were still trying to nettle the captured Guardians and clear their minds. Cut and Dulnas wrestled free and tried to save their nearest friends by shoving away the 'rescue party'. Minor scuffles were breaking out amongst the Guardians.

'Enough of this talk!' One Rochgwar grabbed his mace and swung at Hinx Matr, while Lex Cerberus also tried to protect Hinx from being attacked by Dulnas. Another Rochgwar tried to hold back his mace-wielding compatriot to stop him from damaging the targets for the next talent show.

Guardians fought against Rochgwars. Rochgwars fought against Guardians. Rochgwars fought against Rochgwars. Guardians fought against Guardians. Everywhere you looked, everyone was wrestling with an adversary, and when one fell, another stepped up to take his place.

It was utter chaos.

*   *   *

'Stop it!' cried Robin as the nettles stung. 'Let us go! Why are you doing this?'

'You've been brainwashed. You don't know what you're talking about!' one of Hinx Matr's men said.

'Brainwashed?' said Robin incredulously. 'Could a brainwashed Guardian do this?' he asked, and started singing the full lyrics to *Delton in the Night* at the top of his voice while fights erupted around him.

'You're right, you certainly are Captain Robin and the cure for brainwashing has worked! Guys,' the soldier shouted to their compatriots. This one's recovered. The nettling's worked! Keep going with the others until they respond to it!'

'Nettle rubbing? A cure for brainwashing?' puzzled Heath. 'Did one of you find that out from a Delton Guardians workbook, by any chance?'

'That's right,' confirmed Hinx Matr, in between defending himself from Rochgwar blows. 'I think I flicked through a pile of workbooks in Vei Sirage's quarters and read that in one of them.'

'Okay ...' grinned Heath, a little embarrassed. 'That might have been one of the silly answers I wrote in mine. Vei Sirage's classes are sometimes a bit boring,' confessed the prankster.

The Guardians stopped fighting amongst themselves and engaged the Rochgwars. But they steathily extracted themselves from fighting Rochgwars by turning them against each other.

'Look, Mr Rochgwar! You wanted to hit me to pieces, but your friend next to you disagreed with you and wanted to save me from destruction!' Jack mentioned.

'Ugh?' the Rochgwar paused and looked at his compatriot. *'You no agree with me? No like whad me say? You no my friend?'* The two Rochgwars turned their attention to each other.

The Guardians slipped through the fighting Rochgwars everywhere and exited Lacton.

190

'The Guardians are escaping! Roll out the mega catapults!' ordered Gridie, the catapult commander.

Dear reader, let's imagine a normal-sized catapult. Now double everything – the length, width and height of the frame, the thickness of the platform, the number of wheels, the range, and the number of arms. Now imagine that instead of a rock bucket at the end of each arm, the two arms in this new catapult have, in between them, a big basket that looks like a modern-day skip to hold rocks. A monster of a catapult. Impressive, isn't it? The Rochgwars had four of these, which had been invented by Gridie. Now imagine being hit by all the rocks from one skip-sized rock basket. You would be seriously hurt. Your guts might squish out. For this reason, the mega catapults were sometimes called the Gridie Guts.

All four Gridie Guts were wheeled into position as the whole team of Guardians retreated, while being pursued and harassed by Rochgwars. The Rochgwars that wanted to capture the Guardians unhurt were engaged in combat with them on the slopes. Those that wanted to destroy them were operating the Gridie Guts,

191

ferrying ammunition from the four rock piles within the camp to load the rock baskets. The Rochgwars rotated the Gridie Guts in pairs, firing two while loading the other two. The Guardians found their escape hindered by the awesome firepower of the Gridie Guts as well as the fighting by those chasing them.

'Fire!' each catapult commander ordered. With a sudden *whoosh!* rock baskets sprang forward suddenly and snapped back a split second later as they hit the retaining bar of the frame, sending their cargo of rocks flying over Lacton's walls, where they eventually *thumped!* on the slopes, pinning the Guardians behind a wall of rocks. The whole frames of the Gridie Guts shuddered with every launch. Some Guardians were hit by the rocks, although thankfully not head on, and their armour protected them.

'Oof!'

'Owwwwwer!'

But it wasn't just the Guardians who got hurt. One Rochgwar had been ready to strike Fil when a rock

192

dropped from the sky and right onto him, shattering him into smaller pieces. Three other Rochgwars had surrounded Lex Cerberus when a salvo of rocks hit everything around him.

'Whoa!' he said, surveying the pile of rocks around him and thankful for his lucky escape.

'Fire!' two of the Gridie Guts commanders ordered.

'More rocks! More rocks! Quickly!' the other two hassled their troops to work faster at loading the catapults.

Final Fight

Gravelburn and Eritnorg were still in their own battle for supremacy. They kicked at each other. They ran. They chased. They punched. They chucked stones, rocks, and whatever weapons lay on the ground at the other. Gravelburn hurled a spear at Eritnorg, which the latter deflected away.

'I don't think you'll be able to beat me,' Eritnorg laughed. 'I know lots of moves you don't!'

Eritnorg launched a huge rock at Gravelburn, causing him to duck.

'Oh yeah?' Gravelburn replied. 'How about this?'

Gravelburn picked up a huge rock near one of the Gridie Guts and returned the favour. It hit Eritnorg on the shoulder.
Eritnorg fumed and charged at Gravelburn. 'I'll destroy you until you become like the others last time at Lacton!'

They wrestled. They tussled. Eritnorg seemed to have the upper hand at times, but Gravelburn always seemed to find a way out of trouble.

'You may think you're great, but Gravelburn is always one step ahead!'

'Really?' Eritnorg sneered with contempt.

They continued their battle and eventually Eritnorg managed to trip Gravelburn backwards and throw him to the ground near one of the wheels of the Gridie Guts. He then climbed up the platform and prepared to jump off it, onto Gravelburn. But Gravelburn slid out of the way, so Eritnorg landed *splat!* on the ground instead.

Then Gravelburn climbed up onto the platform, hoping to repeat the same manoeuvre that Eritnorg had tried. He had to duck for an instant as the catapult he was on was put into action to fire its rocks. Luckily, he did – the rock basket briefly occupied the same space his head had just been in. The whole frame shook from the recoil of the rock launch. Gravelburn wobbled unsteadily and before he could jump off, he found two hands grabbing

195

at his ankles. Gravelburn tried to free himself while Eritnorg held on, but the rock basket, returning to its original position to be refilled, hit him on the side of the head and left him dazed. Eritnorg then tugged sharply at Gravelburn's ankles, causing him to fall. Gravelburn was losing the fight.

Eritnorg mounted the platform. Gravelburn was trying to get up but Eritnorg stuck a foot on his chest and pinned him down. Around them the Rochgwars were working hard to refill the catapult's rock basket. 'Faster! Faster! Faster!' the team commander cried. 'Don't let the Guardians get away!'

'So!' laughed Eritnorg. 'One step ahead, eh? Looks like I've got one step on you this time, 'Chosen One'! I'm going to smash you into lots of tiny pieces. This will be the last Gravelburn we will ever see! *Arghahahahahahahahahaha!* Goodbye, Chosen One!'

Dear reader, in case you don't know by now, Rochgwars are stone monsters that regenerate. When they are defeated, they break into pieces, and those that are big enough eventually grow back into

Rochgwars. That's why there always seems to be a never-ending supply of them.

But they can only grow back from rocks that are at least a certain size. If they were broken into pieces that were too small, they cannot regenerate. This is what Eritnorg was threatening to do to Gravelburn – to wipe him out forever, by smashing him into pieces too tiny to regenerate. It would be 'goodbye Gravelburn' forever.

'Be careful up there, sir!' a catapult commander barked out to Eritnorg as the latter slowly drew Gravelburn up to his feet for the finishing blow.

Eritnorg kicked Gravelburn squarely in the chest. Gravelburn had rounded his back slightly but he still felt most of the impact of the kick. It was not enough to break him up though. He fell back, and as he fell he managed to grab the ankle of Eritnorg's kicking leg. Eritnorg was dragged forward, along with Gravelburn's momentum. The two fell right into the rock basket of the Gridie Guts catapult.

197

'Fire!' the commander had shouted as they were falling, and the *whoosh!* of the launch a split-second later sent Gravelburn, Eritnorg and a basket full of rocks flying over the walls of Lacton.

Epilogue

The Guardians eventually made it back to Delton. There, they were welcomed with open arms by Murx Espin and their fellow Guardians. Murx Espin had been worried all the time they had been away, and was glad to see them back safe and sound.

For their bravery in rescuing the captured Guardians from Lacton, Hinx Matr and Lex Cerberus were promoted to master sergeants.

A few nights later, Murx Espin announced that there would be a special dinner that evening to celebrate Power Unit's safe return. At the dinner, he made a special announcement. 'Fellow Guardians, Power Unit have made an important discovery. Lacton is no longer a Guardian stronghold. Now it is controlled by Rochgwars, but we will all pledge to uphold the Guardian name and defend ourselves from all the threats around us!'

The Delton Guardians roared loudly in approval.

Murx Espin then called the Dulnas, Wistan and the members of Power Unit forward.

'These youngsters have demonstrated great mental strength to survive capture and interrogation by the Rochgwars,' he said proudly. 'This is due to the resilience they have developed through training hard. We are all proud of how them. Perhaps, Captain Robin, you might like to tell us about your time there.'

Robin looked aghast. But he quickly recovered and huddled the others together for a brief discussion. Gasps of protest could be heard from Nitro and Jack, before Robin faced the crowd.

'We're going to tell you about our time in Lacton using a song. But before we do that, could you all follow me, and clap your hands six times?' He demonstrated and the crowd followed.

'Now do the last two claps a bit faster than the others.'

Clap clap clap clap clap-clap!

'Now say the words, 'In Lacton in the night!' to the clapping.'

He demonstrated and the audience followed, unsure about what this was going to lead to.

'Keep it going! That's it – keep it going!' Robin encouraged. He waited for the clapping and chanting to establish itself and then urged it to a crescendo by waving his arms upwards, asking for more.

Clap clap clap clap clap-clap!
'In Lacton in the night!'

As the clapping went on, the junior Guardians stepped forward one by one:

Slick:
They said we could go
If we put on a show

Audience: *(clapping)*
In Lacton in the night!

Robin:
I thought it was foul
to perform with an owl

Audience: *(clapping)*
In Lacton in the night!

Ember:
I felt a bit nauseous
So I told myself, "Be cautious!"

Audience: *(clapping)*
In Lacton in the night!

Nitro:
I'm not singing, no I said
I'm not singing

Audience: *(clapping)*
In Lacton in the night!

Heath:
I set out my lace
(Pointing to Dulnas) He fell on his face

Audience: *(clapping)*
In Lacton in the night!

Jack:
I don't wanna do it!
I don't wanna do it!

Audience: *(clapping)*
In Lacton in the night!

Cut:
I thought it was right
To show how we fight

Audience: *(clapping)*
In Lacton in the night!

Fil:
We were a mean bunch
We showed how we punch

Audience: *(clapping)*
In Lacton in the night!

Wistan:
I was very hungry
I dreamt of a turkey

Audience: *(clapping)*
In Lacton in the night!

Dulnas:
I dreamt of lasagne
Er, what rhymes with lasagne

Audience: *(clapping)*
In Lacton in the night!

Dulnas: (continuing)
Lasagne ...
Masagne ...

Audience: *(clapping)*
In Lacton in the night!

Dulnas: (still continuing)
Asagne, Basagne
Casagne, Dasagne

Audience: *(clapping)*
In Lacton in the night!

Dulnas: (still continuing)
Esagne, Fasagne
I can't find anything to rhyme with the word

Audience: *(murmuring)*
In Lacton in the night!

The clapping of the audience, sharp and crisp at the beginning, was now sounding like the cracking of eggs on the floor. Thankfully Murx Espin stepped in and waved Power Unit off before more damage could be done to the audience.

'I also have another announcement to make,' Murx Espin said. 'This evening, the camp chef, Captain Cook, has prepared a special meal for us to celebrate the safe rescue of Power Unit ... '

A special meal! Robin thought excitedly. *Could it be potato rolls?* Oh, how he loved -

'Omelettes!' Murx Espin announced.

*   *   *

The Guardians were not the only ones celebrating that night. The Rochgwars were having some celebrations of their own too. Gratin was now in charge at Lacton, now that Gravelburn and Eritrnorg were no longer there, and he was now the most senior-ranking Rochgwar around. His first instruction was to tell all the Rochgwars there, *'Paaaaaaaaaaaaaaaarty!'* and that night, the Rochgwars danced away, singing:

Me Rochgwar
You Rochgwar
He Rochgwar
She Rochgwar
We all Rochgwars
We all Rochgwars
We make you go 'wah wah'!

The parties went on every night, for many nights. On one of those nights, the full moon climbed high in the sky, illuminating the piles of rocks around the Lacton landscape – rocks thrown up by the Gridie Guts as well as the broken remains of stone warriors on that fateful day.

From one of the rock piles, a pair of legs suddenly kicked out. One by one the surrounding rocks fell to the side as a figure extracted himself from the pile, brushed himself free of dust, before setting off into the distance.

Squeak! Squeak! Squeak!

Printed in Great Britain
by Amazon

22897251R00119